The Pendle Witch Girl
A Witches of Pendle Novella

Sarah L King

Copyright © 2018 Sarah L King

All rights reserved.

ISBN-13: 978-1-9998987-1-7

Published by Ethersay Publishing, Scotland

Cover Design by http://www.selfpubbookcovers.com/FrinaArt

ACKNOWLEDGMENTS

As always, my heartfelt thanks goes to my family for their love and support, especially my husband David who continues to be my rock during the editing and publishing process.

I would also like to thank my draft readers K.J Farnham, Alexandra King and David King for their time, effort and feedback.

Prologue

Spring 1609
'Crumbling Stones'

"Ouch!" Jennet exclaimed as she scraped her knees across the large stones which were strewn across the ground. These piles of rubble were all that remained of the back wall of the out-building now; last winter had been harsh and the old walls hadn't had the strength to resist the relentless frost and biting wind. One day, just after fresh snow had fallen on to the frozen ground, she had wandered outside and round the corner as she usually did and the wall had gone. Just like that - gone. It shouldn't have been a surprise, really. For as long as Jennet could remember, the building had served no purpose other than to sit there, crumbling. She had asked her mother and grandmother repeatedly what it was for and both had shrugged, claiming not to know. Even when she badgered them for an answer, both continued to plead ignorance. She found adults so irritating when they were evasive like that; they probably did know and they just didn't want to tell her. Who cares about old buildings and their uses when you've grown-up things to worry about?

Still, Jennet felt sorry for the old stone hut, sitting there all alone and falling apart. She decided that if the rest of her family weren't interested in finding a use for it, then she would take it upon herself to do so. She would give it a purpose. Last summer, it had been her den, a little house all of her very own, but now that the back wall had gone it didn't make a particularly good or cosy home any more. This spring, she decided, she would play on the rocks instead. That had seemed like a good idea until just a few minutes ago, when she had scraped her knee. Now she had drawn a little blood and her knee ached.

"Mama!" she shouted as she ran back towards her house. She ran inside and slammed the heavy wooden door of Malkin Tower behind her. "Mama!" she called again. "I've hurt my knee! Can you look?"

Slowing her pace and feigning a slight limp, Jennet walked to the back of their cottage, where her mother was sitting in the kitchen near to the hearth, chattering away with her friend, Jennet Preston. On Jennet's lap sat her daughter, Bess, who was wriggling around, dribbling over a piece of soggy bread. Jennet shot the child a disdainful glance.

"Mama, I've hurt my knee," she repeated, offering up her leg for her mother's examination. There was quite a lot of blood now; it had trickled down her shin and settled on her ankle, where it had begun to dry.

Elizabeth Device wasn't amused. "It's nothing, Jennet. Bit of blood is all. No need to make such a fuss," she said, sharply. "Honestly, you're eight years old and still acting like a baby!"

"Shouldn't Grand-mama have a look?" Jennet asked, deciding to pursue the matter of her injured knee and ignoring her mother's jibe. "Grand-mama is good at mending people," she added, smiling at Jennet Preston.

Jennet Preston returned the child's smile. "Yes, your grandmother is good at a great many things," she replied affirmatively. "You are very lucky to have her."

"Grandmother's sleeping," her mother replied. "Please don't wake her. Now, go and play, Jennet," she added, gently but insistently.

"I've no one to play with!" Jennet whinged. "James and Alison are both out, and even when they're here they don't want to play with me. They think they're grown up now, too. Everyone's a grown up except me!" She gesticulated wildly with her arms for dramatic effect. It was a fair point, she thought. Her brother and sister really did think they were too old for her games.

The two women simply laughed at Jennet's outburst. "What a lass you are," her mother said, rubbing her hair affectionately. This gesture was intended to offer comfort but Jennet only found it infuriating.

"Can Bess come and play with me?" Jennet asked, glancing warily at the drooling child. Bess's face was always wet and she couldn't talk much yet, but she could walk and that meant she would do for a friend, for today at least. Maybe Jennet could teach her to climb on the rocks carefully without scraping her knees.

Jennet Preston chuckled. "Bess is too little, Jennet," she replied gently. "In a few years when she's grown a little more, I'm sure she will be your very best friend. Just like your mama is my closest friend," she added, giving Elizabeth Device a warm smile.

"I can't wait that long," Jennet answered rudely. She paused for a moment, allowing the two women to stare at her with confused faces. Jennet enjoyed moments like this, when adults stopped talking about boring things and listened to her. "By the time Bess is old enough to play with me, all the walls on my house will have fallen down and there will be nothing left. I won't need a friend then, if there's nothing left to play with."

Later that day, Jennet watched from behind the front wall of her house as Jennet Preston and Bess finally left. She took care to make sure that she wasn't seen; she liked the sense of watching other people without being spotted. Her brother James had once remarked that she was so good at it, perhaps she could go and spy for the King! The King indeed! James could be so silly at times. What would the King want with a little girl from Pendle?

Jennet watched her mother's friend as she carried her daughter down the hill and disappeared into the distance. She liked Jennet

Preston; she was always kind and friendly to her, but she talked a lot which was no use if Jennet wanted to speak to her mother. With Jennet Preston around, she could never get a word in edgeways. A couple of years ago, which felt like a long time ago to Jennet, her mother's friend had lived at Malkin Tower for a little while. Jennet had quite forgotten all about it, and perhaps would have forgotten forever if her sister Alison hadn't reminded her. Alison liked to talk about people she knew and everything she knew about them, especially if she knew bad things. As young as she was, Jennet knew that if you wanted to know about something bad, you could go to Alison and she would tell you.

"Do you know why Jennet Preston lived here?" Alison had asked mischievously once she knew that her little sister was hanging on to her every word.

"No. Why?" Jennet had replied, her eyes wide with wonder.

"Because she had to run away when everyone in Gisburn found out that she was having Master Lister's baby," Alison answered, her tone matter-of-fact but catty.

"Who's Master Lister?" Jennet had asked innocently.

"A gentleman," Alison replied, tossing her head sharply, as though to emphasise the importance of this man's rank. "And he wasn't her husband. Jennet Preston seduced a gentleman, can you imagine it?" she added with a giggle.

Jennet had been confused. She didn't really understand a lot of what Alison was telling her, but guessed that this Master Lister must have fallen in love with kind, smiling Jennet Preston. That was quite clever of Jennet, she thought, to make a gentleman fall in love with her.

"How did she do that?" Jennet asked.

"Who knows," Alison replied. "Maybe she bewitched him!" she added with a mischievous cackle.

"Alison! You can't say things like that!" Jennet exclaimed.

"Why not?" asked Alison with a casual shrug. "I only mean that she might have cast a love spell. People do spells all the time, for all sorts of things. Look at what Grandmother does. She's started teaching me too, so that I might know spells and remedies for everything, just like she does."

"Can I learn?" Jennet asked eagerly.

"When you're much older," replied Alison haughtily. "And only if you have the gift. Not everyone has the gift, you know. Even if you do have it, Grandmother will want to be sure that you won't use it for ill-wishing before she'll teach you. Ill-wishing is witchcraft."

"I would never do anything bad!" Jennet exclaimed. "I only want to mend people, like Grand-mama."

Despite her pleas, neither Alison nor their grandmother had checked to see if Jennet had the gift. Alison didn't share any of her learning with her younger sister, and no amount of prying or pleading could persuade her to loosen her tongue. Now, sitting in her crumbling den, Jennet was reminded of how much she wanted to have her grandmother's gift and some of her powerful knowledge. She realised, however, that she could still pretend. She could make up her own spells in the safety of her den and pretend that she was turning milk to butter, or making ale taste better. She'd no use for love spells yet, but she could pretend to cure a few sick animals. If she pretended to do all these things now, she was sure that when her grandmother decided she was old enough to learn properly, she would be even better prepared than Alison.

It was almost dark when Jennet decided to venture back indoors that evening. She had been so absorbed in her game of magic that she hadn't noticed the fading light. She approached the door of Malkin Tower with some trepidation, feeling certain that her mother would be waiting behind it, armed with some harsh words and a cross expression. Carefully, she opened the door, trying to prevent it from creaking so that she could sneak in without drawing attention to herself.

To Jennet's surprise, however, the sound which greeted her was not her mother's scolding tone but raised voices coming from the back of the house. Unable to dissuade her curiosity, Jennet crept towards the kitchen and hid around the corner, close enough to hear but out of sight. She immediately recognised the two voices as those of her mother and Alison. She sighed disappointedly. Arguments between her mother and Alison were nothing new; Alison was forever disappearing into the countryside for hours on end, and her mother never knew what she was doing or who she was with. She was about to lose interest and walk away from her hiding place, when something Alison said caught her attention.

"You know what John Robinson says about you?" Alison asked her mother. Even from her hiding place, Jennet could sense the vindictiveness in her sister's tone. She shuddered. She hated it when Alison behaved like this.

"No, Alison," her mother sighed in reply. "Tell me, what does he say?"

"He says you're a whore," Alison spat. "He knows that you had a child with Richard Sellers when my father was still alive."

"Yes, I'm sure he does know that, Alison," replied her mother, forcing her tone to remain even through gritted teeth. "I'm sure everyone round here knows that. You've known about it yourself for a few years now, and I really wish you'd stop bringing it up. She's your sister, Alison."

Jennet's interest began to dissipate. Her mother was right; Alison was always bringing up the fact that she and Jennet had different fathers. Like Alison, Jennet knew that Richard Sellers was her father, and that she only had the Device name because her mother chose not to mark her as different from her siblings. None of this was anything new. She thought about leaving her hiding place again. Perhaps she could go and find her grandmother, or James.

"How do you feel about people calling you a whore, mother?" Alison demanded, recapturing Jennet's attention with her raised voice. "Does it not make you angry? Does it not make you ashamed?"

"Ashamed? Never!" said her mother in response, her voice growing louder now as she became angrier. "No one can understand my actions, no one can understand how I felt at the time, and no one should judge me!"

"So it makes you angry?" Alison goaded. Jennet could sense the pleasure she was taking in riling her mother. She shuddered again, feeling glad now that she was still hiding.

"Yes it makes me angry! A pox on John Robinson, and his brother too! A pox on them both!" her mother screamed.

Silence followed. To Jennet it was a long, worrying silence, since from her hiding place she couldn't see what had happened. Stealthily, she crept towards the door and peered round into the room. There, she could see her mother, sat down, the dog they called Ball spread across her lap. Ball must have come in for scraps before the argument had ensued. Poor Ball, thought Jennet, caught in the middle. He didn't even live here really; he just came in when he felt like a meal and a fuss.

"It's alright Ball," she could just about make out her mother's muttering. "It's alright. We'll show them, won't we? We'll teach them to hold their nasty tongues. I curse the Robinson brothers. I curse them both."

Jennet gasped. This was the first time she'd heard her mother speak in that way. She tiptoed away from the doorway, unseen, and went through to the bedroom where she slipped silently under a blanket. She didn't feel like eating now, she didn't want to see her mother; she just wanted to hide away. After a while she fell into a restless slumber, disturbed by the thought that her mother had just wished away two lives, that the Robinson brothers might suffer dreadful deaths as a result of her words. Tossing and turning, she cried out in her sleep, her dreams plagued by images of death and suffering. In the middle of the night, surrounded by darkness, Jennet awoke suddenly, a sharp gasp of air escaping from her lungs as she sat up straight. In the pitch black silence, a terrible thought suddenly occurred to her. If her mother had the gift, she realised, then she had just used it to ill-wish someone, to throw a curse upon them. Alison's words rang in her ears. Ill-wishing is witchcraft.

Jennet gulped hard. Had her mother just done the work of a witch?

Part One

1610

"She was a very old woman, about the age of Fourescore yeares, and had been a Witch for fiftie yeares. Shee dwelt in the Forrest of Pendle, a vaste place, fitte for her profession: What shee committed in her time, no man knowes"

Thomas Potts, The Wonderfull Discoverie of Witches in the Countie of Lancaster

1

Maundy Thursday 1610
'A Pox on Rain'

Jennet sat down at the little window of Malkin Tower and sighed. She gave the view outside a cursory glance, just long enough to note that the few droplets of rain which had brought her inside moments earlier had now multiplied into a heavy torrent, bouncing relentlessly off the green land. The rain had arrived swiftly after days of spring sunshine, creating that delicious smell that only comes with freshly-soaked grass. The smell of captured sunshine, Grand-mama called it. She didn't know why, nor did she care. She didn't care for rain.

"A pox on rain," she muttered. She said it quietly, though. To say words like that loudly would always earn her a swift hand across the back of her legs. Still, she wished it: a pox, a pox, a pox. If she was God, she would make sure that it never rained.

She rested her chin on her hands and sighed again, louder this time, so that anyone who cared to listen might realise that she was bored. She longed to go back outside, to roam freely across the gentle slope of the hillside upon which her home sat, to play her games away from her mother's and grandmother's watchful eyes. Frustrated, she kicked the stone wall, again and again until pain shot through her toes and made her yelp. Stupid, crumbling home. Stupid rain. Stupid boredom.

"I'm sure I can find you something to do, lass," said her grandmother sleepily.

Surprised, Jennet turned to face the dozing old woman. Grand-mama was rarely ever awake in the afternoons. Mother said that she needed plenty of sleep, that it was important on account of her age and her health. Jennet couldn't imagine anything duller than sleeping for half the day. Except perhaps being awake and stuck indoors while it rained incessantly outside.

Relishing the fact that she now had some company, Jennet shot her grandmother a beaming smile. "Can I fetch you anything, Grand-mama?" she asked sweetly.

The old woman shook her head. "No thank you, lass. Supper is on the hearth. Be a good lass and give it a stir, would you?"

Jennet nodded obligingly and gave the contents of the large pot a cursory mix. Her belly grumbled loudly as the smell of food wafted up her nostrils. She realised that she hadn't eaten that day. As she glanced down at the thin pottage her mouth watered, her empty stomach wishing it was supper time. That was all she wanted; a sunny day and a good meal. It wasn't so much to ask for, really.

Seeing the longing on her face, her grandmother chuckled. "Get yourself a piece of bread," she instructed. "Just a small one, mind, and don't tell your mother."

"Thank you, Grand-mama," Jennet replied, sitting back down at her grandmother's side as she teased the dry, brittle bread apart with her fingers, nibbling it carefully so that it might last longer.

Her grandmother smiled. "You're savouring that," she remarked.

Jennet simply nodded in response. Her mother had once cautioned her against eating too quickly, warning her that she risked a sore stomach or worse, the swift return of her hunger pangs. Jennet had slowed down then, realising that the last thing she wanted to feel was unwell or hungry. It was the one piece of her mother's advice to which she strictly adhered because she had found that it was true; the slower she ate, the longer the food seemed to linger in her gut. For once, it seemed, her mother had been right.

"Where's James?" Jennet asked between mouthfuls, a frown gathering between her curious little eyes. She knew her mother was still out working at the Baldwins' mill and that Alison was out roaming, as her mother called it, but she realised that she hadn't seen her brother today. Like her mother, James had some work, labouring mostly, although it was fairly piecemeal. The only time he was out from dawn until dusk was during the harvest, and even then the work could be sporadic if the harvest had been poor. Consequently, it was not like him to disappear for an entire day.

"He took himself off for the service at St Mary's this morning," her grandmother replied. "I haven't seen him since."

"He went to church?" Jennet asked. "On a Thursday?"

"Aye lass, 'tis Maundy Thursday." Her grandmother's eyes rolled sleepily as she spoke.

"Why didn't we all go, Grand-mama?" Jennet pressed her, keen to keep her grandmother awake with her conversation. For a moment the notion of having gone to church quite appealed to her. It would have been an adventure, setting out across the rolling countryside all the way to Newchurch-in-Pendle. Perhaps she would ask to go with James next time.

The old woman gave a slow laugh. "I'm not well enough to venture far these days."

"Did you used to go to church, Grand-mama?"

Her grandmother shrugged. "Sometimes. I never cared much for it, though. I was raised in the old ways. I'm unaccustomed to the way things are done now." She seemed to choose her words carefully, and Jennet's interest piqued.

"What were the old ways, Grand-mama?" she asked.

Her grandmother smiled and patted her hand. "I'm tired, lass. A story for another time, perhaps."

Jennet watched her grandmother close her eyes before returning to the window. Outside, the rain continued to fall, a heavy torrent battering the side of the old cottage, the water no doubt seeping through the gaps in the aged stonework. It would begin to feel damp inside soon. It always felt damp when it rained.

Jennet stared out of the window, feeling annoyed. No one in her family ever explained anything properly to her. It was always the same; someone would make a remark and, although she would question it, no explanation was ever forthcoming. Jennet pressed her lips together and blew; the coarse sound which followed giving a voice to her frustration. As she listened to her grandmother snoring softly she clenched her fists, resisting the urge to nudge the old woman, to wake her and ask again: what were the old ways? That was today's question, but she had many more. She had so many questions. Jennet tapped her fingers, running through them all in her mind. She had asked most of them in the past, of course, but all had gone unanswered.

"Why do folk call you Old Demdike, Grand-mama?" she had asked once. "What does it mean?"

Her grandmother had given her a small, mysterious smile. "I've had a great many names, lass," she replied. "That's just the one folk have settled upon, I suppose."

Jennet grimaced at her recollection. That hadn't been a proper answer. Even Alison, who was rarely lost for words, had merely shrugged when approached later with this question.

"Some say it means that she's a woman in league with the Devil," Alison had said in the end, hissing the words under her breath.

Jennet had frowned. "But I don't understand. Grand-mama is a good woman. She's a healer."

Alison had offered no further explanation, preferring to leave her sister's confusion hanging in the air like an autumn mist. Jennet sighed. Other matters in their lives confused her too, such as why certain folk in the Forest of Pendle were regarded as friends, but others as mortal enemies. One such family was the Redfearnes, led by a cantankerous old woman called Anne Whittle, better known around the villages as Old Chattox. Throughout her short life, Jennet had caught small snippets of information as those around her exchanged gossip or shared stories. This information had been enough for her to understand that years ago, Old Chattox and her grandmother had begun a dreadful feud, and that this had continued through the generations, with each member of the two families imbued with a deep-rooted hatred of the other. Indeed, she had been raised to dislike Chattox and her two daughters, Bessie Whittle and Anne Redfearne, even though she barely understood why.

"They're evil folk," her mother had told her once. "They're the reason your father's no longer here with us. Thieving, cursing witches, the lot of them."

"What did they do to my father?" Jennet had asked, wide-eyed.

"John Device wasn't your father, Jennet," Alison had interrupted. "You shouldn't confuse Jennet, Mother. It's unkind."

That remark had ended the conversation. Jennet winced now as she considered Alison's sentiment. Her sister had been correct in principle; it was unkind to confuse her, to mislead her, to raise her on a diet of mystery and half-truths. She knew that her sister was right, because she knew how much she longed to know more about her family, its secrets, its trials and tribulations. Instead, she was always left in the dark, left to ponder, left to feel confused. Jennet kicked the wall hard again, pressing her hand hard against her mouth to prevent herself from crying out as pain surged through her toes. The irony of Alison's lecture, of course, was that the one thing she had never been confused about was the nature of her parentage. Alison and her constant, bitter reminders had seen to that.

The rain had continued to fall for the rest of the day, leaving Jennet cooped up indoors. Her mother had arrived home in the late afternoon, weary after a day's labour at the mill. Jennet knew her mother well enough to understand that tiredness made her irritable and so she had made herself scarce, making sure to be quiet and mind her manners, keeping her questions and her chatter to herself. The only remark she made was to ponder James's whereabouts as suppertime approached and there was still no sign of him. It was unlike her brother to be out all day and as the sun began to set, Jennet had felt herself grow worried. Her mother, however, had merely shrugged. He's a grown man now, she had said. He can do as he pleases.

After a supper of watery pottage and stale bread she had crawled into bed, feeling tired despite the day's inactivity. She lay there for some time, dozing, enjoying the luxury of having a bed all to herself before Alison came home and climbed in beside her. She sighed at the thought of her older sister. She was as irritable as her mother; grumpy and short-tempered. They were so alike that it was no wonder that they fell out so frequently. Often Jennet wondered what Alison got up to all day, who she was with and what adventures she was enjoying. Despite Alison's shortcomings, her changeable moods and fiery temper, Jennet secretly admired her. Alison was a free spirit; a little rain never stopped her going out all day, and no amount of cross words from her mother ever prevented her from doing exactly as she pleased.

Sometimes Jennet would wonder if today was the day when Alison didn't bother to come home at all, whether today was the day that she had met a handsome stranger and together they had run away. She knew that this was Alison's wish; her sister had confided this secret to her in one of her softer moments. Jennet had beamed at being taken into her sister's confidence and she had cherished the delicious secret ever since. However, lying there now, alone in their bed, it struck her that life would be much less interesting without her older sister at her side, even if she did take more than her fair share of the bed and blankets. She hoped then that today was just another ordinary day and that her sister would return, tired but elated from her day's pleasures.

It was long after nightfall before Jennet got her wish. She had fallen asleep and had been dreaming about a mysterious land far away from Pendle, a land of rivers running with fire, of snow-capped mountains and dark, endless caves. Fearless as usual, she had just entered one of the many caves when her dream had been rudely interrupted. At first she had taken the noises she heard for one of the many strange, unfamiliar animals she was sure to meet within the cave. However, as she drew further from sleep and nearer to waking, she realised that she recognised her sister's voice. She was talking to someone, her tone animated and characteristically teasing. Curious, Jennet sat upright and drew her ear nearer to the wall, straining to hear.

"Haven't you heard? He's dead," she heard her sister say. Jennet gasped; who was dead, and who was Alison talking to?

"He died yesterday, apparently. It was sudden, or so I heard," Alison continued. "Didn't you argue with him just last week?" she asked. Jennet noticed how she sounded gleeful. She shuddered; she hated it when Alison behaved like a gossiping old crone.

"Yes," came the reply. The voice was quiet but Jennet recognised it immediately as belonging to James. "Yes, we did argue. He promised me an old shirt to wear when I'm labouring but when I went to collect it, he said he'd changed his mind. I have so few shirts as you know, so I suppose I became angry. John was always doing that; saying one thing but doing another."

Jennet heard Alison snort. "John Duckworth is a silly old fool! Or should I say he was, since he's now dead."

"Stop saying that, Alison." James's protest was mild but Jennet sensed anguish in his words.

"Why, James? It's the truth. Why do you care if he's dead?"

"It's an un-Christian thing to do, to speak in that way about someone who has died," James protested feebly.

Alison laughed. "Oh! I forgot - you've spent the whole day on your knees in front of an altar, haven't you?"

"Yes. As should we all," James replied, his voice serious and, Jennet thought, a little strained. She shuddered again; Alison was obviously starting to get to him. "We all have much to beg forgiveness for."

"Do we?" Jennet sensed the challenge in her sister's voice. "And what did you ask God to forgive you for, James?"

"Alison," he said, his voice wavering. "I think the Devil is trying to tempt me. I saw him today, on the road home."

"Oh, James! Is this another one of your far-fetched tales?" his sister mocked.

"No. No! I'm serious Alison. I saw this…this thing, it was shaped like a hare and at first I took it for an ordinary animal, but then it spoke to me, and…"

"What did it say?" Alison's voice was lower now. Jennet's ear began to hurt as she pressed it hard against the wall. She ignored the pain; she was spellbound, desperate to know what the hare had said.

James sighed. "It asked me for the bread which had been blessed at the church. Grand-mama had asked me bring it home rather than taking my share at the altar. No doubt she wanted it for one of her remedies. Anyway, I told the hare that I didn't have the bread, and that I had taken it before the minister as any good Christian should."

"What happened then?"

"The hare grew angry and said that he would pull me to pieces instead." James's tone was fearful at the recollection.

"And what did you say?"

"Nothing. I was too frightened. I marked myself with the sign of the cross and the hare disappeared. I marked myself as belonging to God and all was well again. But don't you see? It must have been the Devil come to take me."

Alison laughed nervously. "Why would you think that, James? Perhaps it was all just a dream, perhaps you fell asleep at the side of the lane for a while and…"

"No!" James cried out. "It was not a dream! I know the Devil came for me, Alison. I know it is because of what I have done…I…it was me who killed John Duckworth!"

A heavy silence descended for a moment. Jennet sat still on her bed, mouth open, heart pounding, waiting for someone to speak.

"What do you mean?" It was Alison who spoke in the end. "Did you ill-wish him?"

"Worse than that," replied James. "I pushed him hard, so hard that he fell to the ground. When I turned to leave, I saw Dandy sitting behind me."

"Dandy?" Alison interrupted him. "Your dog?"

"Yes. I looked at Dandy and he looked back at me. At that moment a voice came into my head, like Dandy was speaking to me. I heard him ask me if I wished for him to kill John Duckworth. I think it was the Devil, Alison, just like today when I saw the hare. I think the Devil took possession of Dandy. He told me that because I had pushed John, it meant that he could have power over him if I willed it. I was so angry that I said yes, I did will it. Now he's dead. He's dead and it's my fault." Jennet's heart sank as she heard her brother begin to sob.

"Oh James, I can't believe what you have done," said Alison. "I can't believe you killed someone! Wait until Grandmother hears of this."

"No, Alison! Wait, I…" James protested. But it was too late; Alison had already opened the cottage door and let it slam shut behind her.

Jennet buried her head under the blankets as Alison came into their little room. She pretended to be asleep, making a concerted effort to steady her breathing as Alison climbed into bed beside her. Her heart continued to pound hard in her chest as her mind reeled over the revelations of the last few minutes. James had murdered someone. Her brother, who she had always thought was so devout and committed to God had, in a moment of anger, called upon dark magic to do his evil bidding. This was worse than ill-wishing. This was worse than anything she had ever encountered before.

Jennet drew her knees up to her chest, hugging herself as she shut her eyes tight. She wished then that she had not eavesdropped, that she had not heard that frightful conversation.

Perhaps that was why her family sought to keep so much from her. They knew that she was just a child. They knew that it was kinder to leave questions unanswered because the truth was too terrifying for her to contemplate. And now, thanks to her own foolish curiosity, she could no longer carry on in blissful ignorance.

Jennet listened as Alison's breathing grew soft and regular. Clearly James's revelations were not about to cause her to have a sleepless night. Jennet sighed. She was wide awake now; she was certain that she would not sleep a wink all night. Her mind was abuzz with new questions. Where did James get his power to harm from? Was it Grand-mama? Was that why folk called her Old Demdike, the devil woman? Jennet frowned. That didn't make any sense. Alison had once told her that Grand-mama's abilities were a gift, but that Grand-mama would only teach you how to use your gift if she was certain you would not use it to harm folk. Why would their neighbours give her such a dreadful name if she was a mere healer?

As she tossed and turned restlessly, Jennet's thoughts settled upon her mother. She recalled that spring night a year ago, when she had heard her mother curse the Robinson brothers. She had tried hard to push all recollections of what she heard that night from her mind, to convince herself that her mother's words had been uttered in anger and nothing more. Even when John and James Robinson had both died within a year of each other, still she had tried to tell herself that it was mere coincidence. Now, given what she had learned about James, the truth seemed inescapable. Her mother had ill-wished them; she was responsible for their deaths.

Jennet gulped hard, wondering again about Alison and Grand-mama, the so-called devil woman and her apprentice. Was Grand-mama really only teaching Alison how to heal, to mix herbs and make remedies, or was she schooling her grand-daughter in darker practices? Was this just one more awful secret that her family were keeping from her? As she began to drift once again towards slumber, her mind came to rest on one terrible thought: if her entire family were capable of such atrocious deeds, what did that mean for her?

2

Easter Day 1610
'Stolen Turves'

"Did you steal her turves?" Elizabeth Device demanded to know, her face flushed with anger and her hands placed defiantly on her hips. Jennet could see her brother shrink back from his mother's rage.

"No, Mother," James replied, his face looking pleadingly at her. "I promise it wasn't me."

"Well, she's telling everyone that it was you, that you've been digging for peat on her land without permission. How do you explain that, if it wasn't you?" His mother persisted with her line of enquiry. Jennet, who was sitting quietly in the corner witnessing the confrontation, could tell that her mother didn't believe him.

James shrugged in response. "What do you think I should do, Mother?" he asked, his eyes downcast.

"I think you should go and see Mistress Towneley and plead your innocence to her. Tell her that you didn't do it, James, because if you don't this could really get out of hand. These rumours about you stealing are all over the villages; it won't be long until they reach the sheriff's ears."

Jennet saw James gulp hard, his eyes wide with fear. The

thought of coming to the attention of the sheriff clearly terrified him, and rightly so. Everyone knew that it rarely ended well for poor folk who provoked men of the law.

"Go right away," Elizabeth urged her son. "Go now and sort out this mess before it's too late."

"But today is Easter Day," replied James, his voice almost a whine now. "Won't I make her angrier if I turn up at Carr Hall today?"

"Oh, a pox on Easter!" exclaimed Elizabeth, clearly at the end of her tether. "I daresay she cannot be any angrier than she is already. Go on; sort out your mess before it's too late. And take your little sister with you," she added, pointing to Jennet, who was lounging restlessly on the floor. "She's been under my feet all day."

Jennet raced to keep up with James as he headed out of Malkin Tower and towards Carr Hall. James had such long legs, being a man of almost twenty now, and Jennet had to take at least three steps for each of his great strides. At least it wasn't a long walk to Mistress Towneley's home in Barrowford, Jennet thought. She should be able to manage it without becoming too tired, even if she had to run most of the way.

"Why does she always do that?" James asked angrily. Jennet wasn't sure if he was talking to her or himself. "Why does she always assume that it's me who has done something wrong? I'm a good son, aren't I? I bring home a wage, I help her at home whenever she asks, and I go to church, well…more often than any of the rest of you! But it's never good enough, is it? She's always so angry with me."

Jennet gave her brother a strange, sideways look. She was unsure what to say. The look on his face was one of guilt, of weariness, of worry; his permanent expression over the last few days. Jennet cast her mind back to the conversation she had overheard just days ago, to James's admission that he had been tempted by the Devil and that he had the death of a man on his conscience. After a couple of restless nights, Jennet had decided to keep what she had heard to herself. She knew that she would be chastised for eavesdropping, and in any case, what would she say and who would she tell? She could hardly tell her mother; after what she had done to the Robinson brothers, she would probably say that old Duckworth deserved it. She wondered for a moment if Alison had told Grand-mama, just as she had said she would, or if she was holding the threat over James's head like the hangman's noose. Jennet shuddered, pushing away the thought. It was little wonder that her brother looked strained.

"Sometimes I think I should just leave Malkin Tower and make my own way in the world, like a man should," James continued.

"No!" cried Jennet. This time she did have a reply for her big brother. "You can't leave, James. I would miss you. Who would tease me, if you weren't there? Mother and Alison aren't funny like you, and Grand-mama is so old, usually I don't understand her jokes."

James looked at Jennet and smiled. "You are silly, sister. Do you know that? You say the silliest things."

Jennet blushed, returning her brother's smile. That was what she liked about James; he could say things like that to her and mean them so nicely. If Alison or Mother called her silly, it was usually in the middle of a telling-off, and was never kindly meant. She looked up at her brother and let out a slight sigh. How could someone so funny and nice have done something so terrible? How could he have the power to kill? None of it made any sense.

"Try to ignore Mama," she said, feeling secretly pleased by the act of offering such grown-up and insightful advice. "Don't let her upset you. She doesn't bother me, and I'm always in trouble for something."

James sighed. "I wish it was that easy," he remarked.

Jennet gave her brother an earnest look. "You can talk to me, James. If something has upset you, you can tell me. You don't have to talk to Alison, you know. I can keep secrets too, even the bad ones."

James smiled and gave her an affectionate pat on the head. "I'll try to remember that," was all he said as they continued along the lane.

They arrived at Carr Hall in the middle of the afternoon, just as the sun was beginning to force its way through the clouds to reveal a beautiful spring day. As the pair walked up the narrow lane towards the Towneley's home, Jennet could hear laughter coming from within. The Towneleys were probably enjoying an Easter feast with family, friends and neighbours. James had been right; today was not a good day to call on them, and their presence would probably only serve to antagonise Mistress Towneley further. Her heart pounding hard in her chest, Jennet took hold of her brother's hand.

"I suppose we're here now," he said, glancing down at her as though looking for reassurance. Normally Jennet would have been well and truly bolstered by the sense of importance this would have given her, had she not felt so terrified. She nodded and attempted a smile, involuntarily squeezing his hand as though to remind him that she was here as well, that she would try to help him as best she could. Poor James; his gaunt face had gone a ghastly shade of white, he looked as though he was about to faint.

James knocked timidly at the heavy wooden door of Carr Hall. They both stood there, hand in hand, for what felt like an eternity before the door slowly creaked open and a man peered around.

"Yes?" the man asked abruptly.

"Good morrow, Goodman," replied James politely, "I'd like to speak with Mistress Towneley, if she's at home?"

Jennet watched as the man looked them both up and down disapprovingly. She felt herself bristle; as young as she was, she was acutely aware of how other folk would often look at her family. This man had a nerve, she thought. He was probably only a servant himself, yet there he was, looking at them both as though they were muck fallen from his boots. It wasn't their fault that their clothes weren't particularly clean, that James's hair and beard were dishevelled and her coif was beginning to fray at the edges. This man would look like that too, if he lived as they did, in a crumbling cottage barely fit for animals, scraping a living from cunning work, labouring and begging.

"May I ask who is calling?" replied the man snootily. Jennet suspected that he knew exactly who they were and why they were here, that he was enjoying taunting them with the charade of formality.

"Please tell Mistress Towneley that it is James Device. I'm sorry to disturb her, but I need to talk to her urgently."

"Very well," replied the man. "Wait there," he instructed, closing the door sharply, leaving them both still standing at the door.

"Do you think she will see us?" Jennet whispered anxiously.

James merely shrugged in response. He looked defeated, his shoulders low and his head bowed. He looked like he had given up, and he hadn't even spoken to Mistress Towneley yet.

"Cheer up," Jennet urged him. "She might see you. She might even believe you."

James shrugged again as the door opened once more. This time it was Mistress Towneley. Jennet instantly recognised that stern expression, framed with the bird-like features of an impeccably straight nose and a pinched mouth, never welcoming, never smiling. She looked sharply at them both.

"Well, well, well," she began haughtily. "I'm surprised you've got the nerve to come here, James Device, after what you've done…"

"Mistress Towneley, forgive me, but that's what I've come to see you about," James interjected. "I didn't steal your turves, Mistress. I don't know who told you that it was me, but I swear on the wounds of Christ that it wasn't." James's tone was pleading; he desperately wanted her to believe him.

"You can swear on whatever you like," replied Mistress Towneley. "It'll make no difference. You were seen. I have witnesses who would swear to it, if I decide to take the matter to the sheriff."

James bristled at the mention of the law. Jennet watched in

horror as he lurched forward, unthinking, taking hold of the mistress's hands, which she had clasped together defensively in front of her belly. "Please, Mistress…" he began.

"Take your hands off me, you brute!" Mistress Towneley shouted. "How dare you lay your hands upon me. Away, away from here! Get out of my sight at once!"

James immediately let go of her hands and turned away, but before he could leave as instructed, Mistress Towneley began to hit him; clumsy thumps to the back and shoulders, lacking in force but filled with humiliation. For a moment, James seemed frozen, as though so shocked by this sudden assault from this woman that he had lost the ability to move. Recognising her brother's plight, Jennet grabbed his hand and used all the strength she could muster to pull on his arm, urging him to move.

"Come, James, come now," she urged.

"Ouch!" James yelled as Mistress Towneley walloped him once more. Responding now to his sister's coaxing, he began to run. Still holding on to him, Jennet struggled to keep up as James ran faster and faster down the lane, until Carr Hall and its angry mistress fell away into the distance.

"James, stop!" Jennet called, panting as she tried to catch her breath. James immediately stopped running and threw himself carelessly down on top of a patch of daffodils which were growing at the side of the lane. Normally Jennet would have winced and scolded him for such a vicious act against beautiful spring flowers, but right now they had more important matters to concern them. Right now, her brother was in a lot of trouble.

"I knew I shouldn't have listened to Mother. I knew I shouldn't have come here today," James said, shaking his head despairingly.

Jennet sat down by his side, sighing heavily as she did so. She didn't answer him; she didn't know what she could say to make him feel better. He was right, after all; coming here today had been a bad idea.

"Now I've made matters worse," James continued. "Mistress Towneley will likely go to the sheriff now; she'll go to him and tell him not only that I stole her turves, but I came to her house and threatened her, I came and put my hands upon her and she had to chase me away."

"You didn't mean it!" Jennet protested. "You didn't mean any of this to happen. It isn't your fault, James."

"I know that, Jennet, but what will that matter to the sheriff? Who is he going to believe, the mistress of Carr Hall or a labourer like me? He'll have me carted off to the assizes without a second thought."

Jennet saw her brother gulp hard, as though struggling to swallow the thought of gaol and a trial, of damning witness statements read out by frightening men of the law. The pair sat in silence for a few moments, both contemplating the gravity of what had just occurred, Jennet resting her head against her big brother's arm. She was tired now; today's events had got the better of her and she longed to be home, safely back at Malkin Tower and tucked up in bed. Closing her eyes, she allowed herself to drift a little, her thumb finding its way into her mouth. She knew it was a babyish habit and she was far from her babyhood now, being almost ten years old. She knew she really must stop it, but it was hard to resist when she was so sleepy. Her grandmother would chastise her for sucking her thumb if she was here. Grand-mama would say…

"Oh!" Jennet gasped, suddenly sitting upright as an idea occurred to her. "Grand-mama! Of course, James! Grand-mama could help."

"Grand-mama?" James replied, furrowing his brow. "How?"

"She might have a spell. Alison says Grand-mama has spells for all sorts of things. Maybe she could cast a spell to make Mistress Towneley forget about her turves," Jennet suggested, trying her best to be helpful.

"Grand-mama can't make people forget things!" James exclaimed, his irritation now evident. He threw his arms up in the air in a despairing gesture. "Really, Jennet, what do you know of what our grandmother can do, anyway?"

Jennet's face flushed with anger at James's cruel remark. It was so unlike him to speak to her in that manner. "I know a lot!" she retorted indignantly. "Grand-mama helps people. She could help you, too!"

"Oh, really? What do you suggest then, Jennet? Do you suggest that I ask her to make a picture? Yes? Well, that would see to the problem, wouldn't it?"

Jennet frowned at her brother. "What picture?" she asked.

James returned her frown, his furrowed brow dissolving quickly into a look of horror as it dawned on him that Jennet had no idea what he was talking about. "Forget it, Jennet. Forget I said anything," he replied, the realisation that he had just given away a terrible secret etched all over his worried face.

"No, I won't forget it!" yelled Jennet angrily. "You can't say things like that and not explain yourself, James. What do you mean, Grand-mama makes pictures? You must tell me or else I will go home and ask Mama."

James gasped. "No! Don't do that! She will know that it was me who told you, and she's angry enough with me as it is," James paused and gave his sister a considered glance, followed by a heavy sigh. "If I tell you, do you promise to breathe a word to no one?" he asked solemnly.

"Of course, James, I won't tell a soul," she swore.

"Grand-mama once told me that it's possible to harm someone by making a model of them from clay and then damaging it," James explained.

"What do you mean, damaging it?" Jennet pressed her brother for more information.

"Burning it, or sticking pins in it, or even burying it. All these things would cause pain to the person you wanted to hurt. If you went far enough, you could even kill them," he added, whispering those final, terrible words.

Jennet's eyes were wide with wonder and amazement. "Who does Grand-mama make pictures of?" she asked.

"She says she doesn't make pictures," James replied. "She told me that she knows how to do it, but that it is dark magic, that it should not be used. Do you want to know who does make pictures?" James asked, a little smirk gathering in the corners of his mouth. He was enjoying himself now, his humiliation at the hands of Mistress Towneley forgotten for a moment as he captivated his little sister with magical tales.

"No, who?" prompted Jennet.

"Old Chattox and Anne Redfearne. Grand-mama says everyone in the West Close fears that pair of witches and their clay pictures," remarked James.

"Oh," replied Jennet, slightly disappointed. Everyone in Pendle knew what Chattox and her daughter were capable of. If there was ever a sudden death, or a bout of sickness in the local animals, Grand-mama said that you could be sure Chattox was responsible. The revelation that she made clay pictures too was hardly surprising, hardly interesting at all. However, the revelation that Grand-mama knew how to make them was of interest. Jennet thought again about her grandmother's nickname; Old Demdike, the devil woman. Had Grand-mama made clay pictures in the past? Could she harm people, if she so chose? Jennet shuddered as she thought again of John Duckworth. Had James inherited her power to harm?

"Do you think you might have harmed Mistress Towneley, James, when you touched her?" she asked, choosing her words carefully.

James looked at her, his eyes wide, his cheeks red. "What do you mean, Jennet?" he asked, his words slow and deliberate. "What are you talking about?"

"I heard you telling Alison about John Duckworth."

James's stare grew wider still, the whites of his eyes seeming to pop out at her. Jennet couldn't decide whether his expression was fearful or menacing. "You shouldn't be listening to other folk's conversations."

"Do you really think you killed him?"

James clapped his hand over her mouth. "Keep your voice

down!" he said, looking around them. "You never know who's listening! I don't know, Jennet. I don't know. All I know is what I heard and what I said in reply. A few words spoken in anger, that's all. I didn't mean it. God forgive me, I didn't mean it." He let his hand fall away from her mouth as he began to sob.

Jennet looked at her brother, open-mouthed, unsure again what to say to comfort him. "You're not the only one," she said in the end. "I've heard Mother ill-wish two people, and now they're both dead."

James looked up. "Who?" he asked, sniffling.

Jennet drew a deep breath. "I remember hearing Mother tell Ball that she cursed James and John Robinson."

"You really should stop listening to other folk's conversations," James scolded. "I think it's time we went home," he said, getting to his feet.

"Do you really think the Devil possessed Dandy?" she couldn't resist asking. She had to know. "Do you think he might have possessed Ball as well?"

James did not answer her. He continued to walk quietly homeward, leaving Jennet to ponder whether their dogs were really just dogs or something altogether more powerful and frightening.

3

**Autumn 1610
'Two Witches Together'**

Jennet skipped gleefully along the lane, her worn boots battering through the sea of colour created by the fallen leaves. Breathlessly she hummed a tune; it was an old and familiar one which her grandmother liked to sing, a cheerful melody forever etched on her memory, reminding her of warm fires and hugs and home. It was a song she kept for when she was happy, and today she was happier than she had ever been. It had been a long, hot summer, the days seemingly endless and filled with possibility. She had spent most of her days outside, playing games around what remained of her old stone hut until, tired and sweating, she had sought refreshment in the cool waters of the nearby stream.

She had been alone, mostly, but she had kept busy, and that was the most important thing. She liked to be busy; if she was occupied then she didn't have time to wonder about the things which bothered her, to worry about her family and the things they might have done. Instead, she allowed herself to have fun, to bask in the sunshine and apply her imagination to her games instead of letting it run wild with her fears. This summer had undoubtedly done her a lot of good and even now, as the Forest of Pendle succumbed to autumn and the bad weather beckoned, Jennet still felt lively. It was hard to resist such happiness when there was so much to enjoy.

"Are you going to stop and wait for me? Mother said not to let you out of my sight," James scolded.

Jennet spun on her heel as she ground to a halt. "Well, it's not my fault that you're slow and old!" she teased.

"Very funny," James replied, not taking her bait.

Jennet gave him a small smile before resuming her skipping, slower this time. She resolved to be obedient; after all, James wouldn't agree to bring her on his adventures if she wasn't. Today they had been to Padiham – after the harvest, James had found himself out of work and with winter looming it was crucial for him to find employment. He had tried the usual villages and the usual places without success so, in desperation, he had been forced to go further afield to try his luck.

Unfortunately, Padiham had proved equally fruitless and now they were heading home, empty handed and unsure what the future would hold. Not that any of this could quell Jennet's good mood. After all, the sun still shone and the lanes were still dry – winter was a good while away yet, time enough for James to find work. And besides, if he didn't, what was the worst that could happen? What did a little more poverty really mean when you were already so very poor?

"Mother's not going to be happy if she's the only one bringing in a wage," James remarked, as though answering Jennet's unspoken question. "Winter will be a struggle. We already survive on so little – I think there will be days when we cannot afford to eat at all."

"Hmm," Jennet pondered, kicking the leaves with her toes. "It's alright – I'm used to being hungry. You've tried your best, James," she added, flashing him her sweetest smile.

"I just wish there was something else I could do!" James threw himself down at the edge of the lane, slumped and defeated.

"Perhaps there is," Jennet ventured, sitting beside her brother.

"Like what?"

"You could use magic. Grand-mama can turn milk to butter, just imagine what else she could do…"

"Yes, she can make one thing into another, Jennet," James answered her, exasperated. "She can't make something out of nothing; none of us can. If she could we wouldn't live in that crumbling house, poor and starving."

"I suppose."

"You really are a silly little girl sometimes."

Jennet rose to her feet, hands placed indignantly on her hips. She could feel herself growing angry; she wasn't used to James speaking to her so unkindly. "No I am not! You're the one whose ill-wishing can…can…" Jennet hesitated, faltering over her words.

James stood up, his tall, skinny frame towering over her. "Can what?" he prompted, his voice challenging.

Jennet swallowed hard, remembering the things that she had spent the summer trying to forget. "John Duckworth, Mistress Towneley…they're both dead, James."

Her brother shook his head as he took a step back. "I don't want to talk about this, Jennet. Not with you, not with anyone."

"Why not?"

James put his head in his hands. "I've done terrible things. Dreadful, unforgiveable things. I can't control it, Jennet. I can't stop it."

"You can't stop what?" Jennet probed further, a frown etched on her face.

"The voices. The voices which come into my head, telling me what to do, encouraging me. It's like the animals are talking to me, Jennet."

"Which animals?"

"Any animal, but mostly Dandy. I hear Dandy speaking to me all the time. Except it's not Dandy, not really. It's the Devil. I know it is."

The mention of that name made Jennet shudder. "If it's the Devil, you should ignore him. Don't do his bidding. Say a prayer instead, or make the sign of the cross, just like Grand-mama does."

James gave her a grim smile. "If only it was so easy. It's hard to explain, but it's like his voice fills my head, taking over me completely, filling me with such hate and anger. It is as though I am not myself. Before I know it, I have done something, or agreed to something that I shouldn't. Before I know it, someone else is dead."

Jennet stared at her brother, wide-eyed, his sombre confession forcing her into silence. Until now she hadn't realised that it was so bad, how little control James had over himself and what was happening to him. Her eavesdropping and probing over the previous months had led her to believe that whilst her brother might have committed murder, it was his own choice, carried out with the use of his own magic. Now, whilst the prospect of James murdering through his own volition was still frightening, the idea of him being the Devil's powerless pawn suddenly seemed much, much worse.

"What did you do to Mistress Towneley, James?" Jennet's voice was barely a whisper.

James's face turned a ghostly shade of white. "I told you; it was Dandy."

"What did Dandy tell you to do?"

"A couple of days after we visited Carr Hall, Dandy spoke to me. He said that I was right to be angry, that Mistress Towneley should not have treated me so unkindly. He told me that there was a way to make her pay for what she had done."

Jennet's eyes widened. Her breath caught in her throat and she clapped a hand over her mouth, suppressing a cough.

"Dandy suggested that I should make a picture of Mistress Towneley, that I should craft it from clay and dry it out by the fire," James continued. "He told me that after that I should crumble the picture, bit by bit, and that by the time the whole thing was crumbled away, Mistress Towneley would be…gone." James's face grew pale and he swallowed hard.

Jennet shook her head slowly, unable to believe what she had just heard. "But Grand-mama told you making pictures is dark magic, James. Surely you didn't listen to Dandy? Surely you didn't do it?"

James gave a feeble nod. "I did. I was so angry; it was like I couldn't stop myself. I told you, I can't control any of this – the voices, the rage, none of it."

"You need to tell Grand-mama," Jennet answered, her voice barely a whisper. "She will know what to do. She will know how to stop this."

"Oh Jennet, you foolish child!" James scoffed. "Even Grand-mama can't defeat the Devil himself. None of us can."

Jennet frowned at her brother, an indignant pout growing on her lips. She was not a fool. She might be young and have a lot to learn about the world, but she knew what was right and what was wrong. Listening to the Devil when he speaks through a dog, uttering curses, making pictures, killing people…it was all wrong.

"You could have ignored Dandy, James," she replied. "You could have told him that you wouldn't do those things. You could have said a prayer and sent the Devil away." She turned her back on James and began to walk away.

"I tried that!" he called after her. "Time and time again I tried. He wore me down, Jennet. In the end I couldn't resist what he was offering. All that power. All that vengeance. And now I have to live with what I have done."

James's final words stung Jennet's conscience and she spun around to see him looking at her, guilt weighing heavily in his eyes. She walked back towards him, her hand outstretched to take his. She couldn't stay angry with him for long. He might have done terrible things, but he was still her big brother.

"Do you think you're a witch now, James?" She whispered the question, the dreadful words making her voice tremble.

James shook his head. "No," he replied. "I'm just a weak person who has done awful things. I have listened to the Devil and let him instruct me so that I could have my revenge. I have done what a lot of folk would have done in anger. But I'm not a witch."

Jennet furrowed her brow. "So you won't do anything like this again? You'll ignore Dandy next time he speaks to you?"

James looked at her blankly, as though he wasn't hearing her question. Then he looked away. Jennet gave a small sigh. Clearly James had decided that the conversation was over, that he wasn't willing to discuss this with her anymore. For all that she loved him, at times he was just as bad as Mama and Grand-mama.

James glanced around him. "Jennet, do you know where we are?" he asked, his eyes growing wide.

"Near Higham, of course," she replied. "I know this country as well as you do. Why?"

"And what's in Higham?" James asked her. "And more to the point, who lives at West Close, just over there." He waved his fingers vaguely into the distance.

Jennet gasped. "Chattox," she replied, her voice a spellbound hiss. "James, we had better get home. Grand-mama is always talking about the terrible things she's done."

James laughed. "Oh no," he said. "All your talk of witches has given me a better idea. You've never seen Old Chattox, have you?"

Jennet shook her head. No, she hadn't, and she wasn't sure that she wanted to either.

"I think it's time you saw what a real witch looks like," he said to her, taking hold of her hand and guiding her off the lane. "Then maybe you can put all this nonsense about me out of your head, once and for all."

Half-horrified and half-enthralled at the prospect of this new adventure, Jennet followed her brother. Not that she had much choice; he was bigger and stronger than her and maintained a tight grip on her tiny arm as he strode along. The thought of seeing this evil old witch made Jennet's heart pound hard in her chest. Chattox was dangerous. She could harm people; she could kill people. But then again, Jennet reminded herself, so could James. No amount of staring at a wicked old hag was going to help her forget about that.

They arrived at Chattox's cottage on tiptoes, heads lowered, creeping stealthily towards a rear window in an effort to avoid detection. The cottage was a sorry, decrepit building, not dissimilar in condition to Malkin Tower, although it was much smaller. Jennet wondered, not for the first time, why if women like Chattox and her Grand-mama were so powerful they couldn't put their magic to better uses. She decided there and then that if she was ever fortunate enough to have these gifts, she would conjure herself a palace fit for a Queen. There would be no crumbling, draughty building to live in if Jennet Device ever became a cunning woman.

"Look!" James hissed. "There she is."

Jennet peered over the windowsill and looked at the old woman for the first time. She was small and frail, much like Grand-mama, and she shuffled around her little cottage, leaning heavily on a rickety stick. Sitting near her was a younger woman who Jennet guessed was her daughter, Anne Redfearne. She knew from the snippets of stories she'd heard at home that Chattox lived with her daughter and her daughter's husband, Thomas. She also knew that both Chattox and her daughter were witches. Jennet stifled a gasp, ducking her head back down and leaning against the wall.

"Two witches together," James whispered. "I wonder what they're up to."

"Doesn't look like much to me," Jennet whispered back. "It's almost dinner time. Maybe they're getting ready to prepare a meal." Her stomach growled hungrily at the thought of food.

"Looks more like they're making clay pictures to me," James replied.

Against all her better instincts Jennet sat back up and took another look. It certainly looked like Anne Redfearne was making something, her posture hunched intently over a plain wooden table. "It could be anything." Jennet gave a small shrug.

"Or it could be dark magic," James said, his eyes transfixed on the scene in front of him.

Jennet bit her lip, irritated by her brother's macabre fascination. If Chattox and her daughter were making pictures, then she didn't see how this was any different to what James had done. Of course, she didn't dare to say it.

The Pendle Witch Girl

"Do you think the Devil talks to Chattox and Anne Redfearne too, like he talks to you?"

James frowned and shifted on the ground. "I don't reckon he needs to," he muttered. "They hardly need tempted. They have plenty of misdeeds to keep them busy. Do you know what they did to Robert Nutter?"

Jennet shook her head slowly. Of course she didn't; no one ever told her anything.

"A long time ago, before you were even born," James began, being careful to keep his voice hushed, "Anne had an affair with a man called Robert Nutter."

"What does that mean?"

James paused, shaking his head slightly as though he was remembering his audience. "It means she fell in love with him even though she was married. But it didn't end well. Anne and Robert had a falling out, which made Anne very upset. In revenge she got her mother, Old Chattox, to put a curse upon him. By the following Candlemas Robert Nutter was dead."

"That's terrible," Jennet gasped. "Anne should never have loved Robert in the first place. What about poor Thomas?"

"Indeed," James replied with a chuckle. "Mind you, I wouldn't get too hung up on all that. You wouldn't be here at all if it wasn't for such…" he drew a short breath, searching for the right word, "well, indiscretions."

Jennet felt her cheeks redden. As young as she was, she understood his meaning perfectly well. It wasn't like James to bring up her parentage and his reference to it stung her like a wasp in late summer. She looked down at the ground, unsure which emotion she felt more keenly – anger or shame. She knew fine well that she was born because, for a time at least, her mother had loved someone else. She knew that she was not John Device's child, that she had been born out of wedlock. She knew that she was a bastard. She wished that everyone would stop reminding her. She wished that they would stop holding it against her.

"Ah! A Device imbecile and a little runt!" came a voice from behind them.

Jennet gasped and jumped up in surprise. They had been so busy speculating at what was going on inside Chattox's cottage that they had neglected to ensure they weren't seen from the outside. Jennet spun around to see a woman standing behind her, eyes wide with fury, hands placed firmly upon her hips. At least, Jennet thought she was a woman, although in truth only her small stature and delicate, almost pretty features marked out her sex. Other than that, she was the strangest-looking woman Jennet had ever seen; no coif, no bodice, no petticoat, no women's clothes at all, in fact. Instead she wore a pair of filthy hose and a loose, equally grubby shirt, her uncovered head adorned only with a curly brown mass which ran wild on the breeze.

The woman caught Jennet's eye. "What are you looking at?" she growled.

Jennet turned to her brother. "Who is she?" she mouthed.

"Well if it isn't Bessie Whittle," James said, giving his sister a half-reply. "Keeping busy with your thieving, I daresay," he added, his tone uncharacteristically bold.

"At least I keep busy. I hear you're out of work again. Little wonder – who'd employ a half-wit like you?" Bessie retorted.

Before Jennet could try to stop him James lunged forward, his great height towering over Bessie, his face staring down at hers. "Say that again and I'll…"

"You'll what?" Bessie replied, returning his hard stare. "Stand down, James Device, you're no man. Look at you, filled with fear, just like your father!"

"Don't you dare mention my father. I know what your mother did, I know how she…"

Bessie put up her hand, allowing it to hover in front of James's face. Behind it, Jennet thought she saw her brother flinch. "No. You think you know, but in fact you don't know anything. You've been told a pack of lies, James Device. All these years spent living with that vindictive old hag Demdike have poisoned your mind."

On hearing those words Jennet jumped to her feet. It was bad enough hearing her brother being insulted, but listening to her grandmother's good name being abused was a step too far. "My grand-mama is a great woman!" Jennet yelled. "She does good magic. She is a healer. She is nothing like your grandmother. It is Chattox who is the evil old witch!"

Bessie Whittle looked at her, an amused smile spreading slowly over her face. "The little bastard speaks," she remarked, her tone goading. "Sounds as though the little bastard has been fed a diet of lies as well. Well, little bastard, here's a thought for you to take away with you today: if my grandmother knows any spells or curses, if she knows how to heal and also to harm, how do you think she came by that knowledge? Who do you think taught her? Old Mother Demdike, of course. The most notorious witch in Pendle."

Jennet stepped back in horror, pressing her back up against the stone cottage wall. "No," she whispered. "No, it's not true, it's…"

Behind her Jennet heard a loud bang. She spun around to see a horrid, wicked face peering through the window, its mouth twisted, its eyes filled with fury as it shook a violent fist in her direction. For a moment Jennet was mesmerised by the sheer horror of its features; the deep brown eyes dark with spite, the yellow, crumbling teeth, the lines of age etched like chasms on its haggard, grey face. It was awful. It was otherworldly. It was evil.

"Chattox," she breathed.

Behind her she felt James reach out and grab her hand. "Let's go!" he cried.

Jennet didn't need to be asked twice. She set off, running as fast as her little legs could carry her.

"That's right – run away, just like the cowards you are!" Bessie called.

Jennet kept running, not daring to look back. She tried desperately to keep up with her brother's enormous strides even when her muscles ached and every last breath was spent. She ran and ran, terrified of being left behind. Terrified of being caught. Terrified, she realised, of being bewitched.

"You can't outrun Mother's magic!" Bessie Whittle's taunt echoed on the breeze.

Jennet's pace faltered for a moment. Of course they couldn't. No one could escape from the clutches of malevolence; no one could escape the Devil's work. No one, she thought, except perhaps her own grandmother who, if Bessie was to be believed, was both the greatest healer and the greatest witch that Pendle had ever seen. Jennet frowned, trying to make sense of what she had just heard. It couldn't be true, could it? Grand-mama did not dabble with dark magic, Jennet reminded herself. Grand-mama only ever used her gifts to help and to heal. If Chattox knew how to do such abominable things, she must have learned them somewhere else. By telling her that Grand-mama had a hand in malign magic, Bessie Whittle was just trying to make trouble. Jennet picked up her pace again, determined to outrun Chattox and her family. Determined, more than anything, to outrun the doubt which plagued her mind.

Once they reached the lane, James came to an abrupt halt. Jennet stopped just behind him, daring finally to turn around. Mercifully, Chattox's cottage was now out of sight, and there was no sign of Bessie, Anne or the old witch herself pursuing them. Jennet let out a heavy breath; part-relief, part-exhaustion.

"I think we lost them," James declared with a smile, clearly enjoying the thrill.

Jennet shot her brother a stern glance. "That was dangerous, James," she scolded. "Imagine what Mama would say."

James merely shrugged. "You agreed to come. Besides, I wouldn't mention this to Mother, if I was you."

"Oh but James, we must! You heard the things Bessie Whittle said, about Grand-mama, about Father..." she paused. "What did Chattox do to Father, James?"

"He wasn't your father."

Jennet clenched her fists. She could feel her face begin to redden, the heat of temper climbing from her neck to her cheeks. "Why does everyone always say that?" she asked, stamping her feet.

James shrugged. "Because it's true. Richard Sellers is your father."

Jennet winced at the mention of the name. It had been flung at her so many times that it ought to feel familiar by now and yet there was always something odd about its sound; something absent, something unknown. "I've never even met Richard Sellers," she replied quietly.

"Aye well…you never met my father either," James retorted, emphasising his words.

Jennet felt her hackles rising once again. She folded her arms, giving her brother a scornful glance. It was true of course; John Device had died before she was even born and although no one would tell her exactly what happened to him, she knew enough to guess that Chattox and her magic had something to do with it. She gave a small sigh. A child with two fathers and she knew neither of them. No wonder Bessie Whittle had taken great delight in calling her a little bastard.

James's indifferent stare melted into an affectionate smile as he saw the sullen look upon her face. "Cheer up, little one," he said, swinging a long, slim arm over her shoulder. "Time to go home. Let's get safely away from these hags and witches, once and for all."

Jennet glanced over her shoulder. "A pox on Chattox, "she muttered. "A pox on Anne Redfearne and a pox on Bessie Whittle, too."

"Aye, a pox on them," repeated James, taking her by the hand. "Well, perhaps you'll get your wish. Perhaps you've just cursed them all."

Jennet looked up at her brother, wide-eyed. She had never considered that her words might hold any power. "Do you think so?"

James shrugged. "Who knows," he replied. "Although you are a child born in sin. I reckon that makes it at least possible. For all we know, little Jennet Device could grow up to be the evilest witch Pendle has ever seen!"

He nudged her arm mockingly and then, laughing, ran off down the lane, expecting her to pursue him. It was a game they'd played a hundred times before, one which Jennet normally relished, but not today. Today, she was aghast. Today, she was paralysed by her brother's words. A child born in sin. A little bastard. A little runt. Yes, she was all of those things; she knew that, and had known it ever since she was old enough to understand. But did that mean she was capable of dark magic, of wielding power, of doing evil? Did that mean that she too was a witch?

And more to the point, Jennet thought as she sauntered along the lane, what would she do if it did?

4

Christmas 1610
'Poor Little Wretch'

Jennet tucked herself into a corner, a cup of stolen ale clutched tightly in her hand. The drink was a strong brew, far stronger than the usual small ale, and it made her feel light-headed. Her mother had told her earlier that she was only allowed a small amount, but that was before she had drunk a lot of it herself; too much, in fact, to notice what her young child was doing. So Jennet had helped herself to a large cup and had drunk it down with a keen thirst. It was disobedient, she knew that, but it was also Christmas, so why shouldn't she have a little fun? After all, everybody else was.

Jennet shuffled around, trying to better hide herself from view. The atmosphere inside Malkin Tower was raucous, the Devices' festive gathering giving friends and neighbours a good excuse to indulge in some revelry. Everywhere she looked there were people laughing, dancing, stumbling around. Some were even sleeping, the combination of food, drink and excitement clearly proving to be too much for them. Indeed, it had almost proven too much for Jennet and if she was honest with herself, she now felt a little bit sick. She rubbed her aching tummy tenderly, feeling sorry for herself. Who could blame her for eating so much mutton, for drinking some of the strong ale? Who could blame her for enjoying the feeling, for once, of not being hungry? It was a cruel world and a cruel God, she thought, to make her suffer for it now.

"Don't let Mother see you with that ale," Alison's voice shot across the room.

Jennet gulped down the last drop in defiance. "What ale?" she retorted.

"Indeed." Alison danced over, looking more than a little unsteady on her feet. "You'll be asleep soon after drinking all that."

"Shan't!" Jennet cried. "I will stay up as long as the rest of you."

Alison slumped down beside her sister, emitting a little sigh. "Well I won't be staying up all night," she replied. "I'm bored already. There is absolutely no one of any interest here whatsoever."

Jennet nodded in agreement. Malkin Tower was full of her mother's and grandmother's friends but no one of her own age. Even Jennet Preston, who could normally be relied upon to bring her daughter Bess, had turned up on her own. "Who do you wish was here?" she asked. "One of the folk you see when you go out all day?"

Alison's cheeks began to colour. "Never mind," she replied, typically secretive when it came to her social life. Their mother always complained that she never knew where Alison was or who she was with all day long.

"Mama says you'll end up with child," Jennet said, repeating one of her mother's more recent complaints. "I heard her say so to Grand-mama."

Alison shot her sister a warning glance but said nothing further. The sisters sat in silence for a few moments. Jennet fidgeted uncomfortably, her belly groaning in protest at the heavy ale and rich food.

"You shouldn't have had that ale," Alison remarked. "Mother told you that you're too young to drink it."

Jennet leaned into the stone wall, too weary to argue. "Tell me a story, Alison," she said, her thumb creeping up towards her mouth.

"Tell me something to help me forget my belly ache."

"Well…" Alison began, considering her words. She could never refuse a request for a story. "Did you hear what John Moore has been saying?"

Jennet shook her head. "Who's John Moore?"

Alison threw her sister a disapproving look. "Really, Jennet? Don't you know who anyone is? John Moore is a gentleman from Higham. Anyway, that's not important, what is important is what he's accused Old Chattox of."

"Chattox," Jennet whispered. Her heart fluttered nervously at the recollection of her brief encounter with that old witch, her horrid face, her hateful stare. She had kept the story of what happened that day between her and James, just as he'd asked her to, but burying the secret hadn't stopped the memory of it springing to the fore every time that dreadful name was mentioned. "What has Chattox done now?"

"Bewitched John Moore's ale, apparently. I can believe it, as well. It's not like she hasn't done it before."

At the mention of ale Jennet's stomach let out an unpleasant growl. "Really?" she asked, looking down at her empty cup.

Alison threw back her head, laughing. "Don't worry, Jennet! She hasn't bewitched yours! You've just drunk too much of it, that's all. Anyway, no doubt the old hag is furious with Master Moore. I wouldn't be at all surprised if he drops dead quite suddenly after this."

Jennet shuddered at Alison's coarse choice of words. "I wish you wouldn't say things like that, Alison."

Alison shrugged. "Why not? It's true. That's all Chattox does: exact revenge. Vengeance is what she lives for. This family knows that better than anybody."

"Do you mean with what happened to Father. To your father, I mean?" Jennet asked.

"Of course I do," Alison snapped. "That evil witch killed my father."

Jennet looked at her sister, open-mouthed. Finally, words to confirm what she had long suspected; words from a tongue loosened by ale and flung out carelessly into the air. Words which prompted so many more questions, questions which Jennet would have asked there and then, were it not for the tears which she could see gathering in the corners of her sister's eyes. Some questions, she realised, would have to wait.

"Mama looks happy tonight," she said, trying to find a cheerier topic.

"She's always happy when her dear best friend comes over," Alison scoffed. "She's like a different person altogether when she's here."

Jennet tried not to wince at Alison's bitter tone. "Do you mean Jennet Preston?" she asked.

"Who else? Gisburn's very own whore. Why do you think she spends so much time over here? It's not like she's got any friends in her own village."

"Mama will scold you if she hears you using words like that," Jennet retorted.

"Well it's true," Alison hissed. "I told you about Master Lister, didn't I?"

Jennet nodded eagerly. "Yes. I remember you telling me that Master Lister fell in love with Jennet, that they had a baby. Bess is their baby."

Alison gave Jennet a sideways glance. She reached up to the table and grabbed another cup of ale. "Is that all I told you?" she asked, taking a sip.

"Yes," Jennet replied, her thumb creeping towards her mouth once again. She could sense another story was coming.

"Well, that isn't the whole sorry tale. Master Lister is dead, Jennet. Died in church on his son's wedding day, in front of all their family, all their friends, and all their servants. Can you imagine that?"

Jennet shook her head. "Poor Jennet Preston," she replied. "She must have been so upset."

"It's worse than that," Alison replied. "As he lay dying, Master

Lister cried out for Jennet, asking her to come to him, declaring his love for her. In front of his wife and his children – in front of everyone! It was the talk of the villages for weeks afterwards. Jennet Preston was well and truly disgraced. That was why she ran away and lived with us for a while, until her husband took her back anyway."

"That was really nice of him to do that," Jennet said half-heartedly. Her eyelids were growing heavy and she could feel herself begin to drift.

"It was more than she deserved," Alison retorted.

Alison's sharp tone nudged Jennet back from the edge of slumber. "You really don't like Jennet Preston, do you Alison?" she asked, her voice small and weary.

"No," she said, looking across the room at where her mother's friend now sat, smiling as she talked to other guests. "I don't like her at all."

"Why not?" Jennet probed. "Is it because she had Master Lister's baby?"

Alison shook her head but kept her eyes fixed on the object of her disdain. "That's why others don't like her. That's why folk in Gisburn don't like her and why the Listers don't like her. But that isn't what bothers me."

"What, then?"

Alison took a deep breath. "I don't like her because she makes our mother happy and happiness is the last thing our mother deserves."

"Alison! That's a horrid thing to say," Jennet gasped. "Why don't you want Mama to be happy?"

Alison gulped down the last of her beer, wiping her mouth with the back of her hand. She turned her disdainful gaze on to her younger sister who sat looking at her, wide-eyed and open-mouthed. "You of all people should know why," she replied. "The reason I hate her is the same reason that you're here, Jennet. It's the reason that put you on this earth and my father in his grave."

"But you said Chattox killed Father…your father."

"Chattox might have done the magic but it was our mother who broke his heart when she went with that man Sellers," Alison replied. "She is a whore, just like Jennet Preston. It's no wonder they get on so well."

This time it was Jennet who felt the tears prick in the corners of her eyes. "You have a wicked tongue, Alison Device – a wicked tongue and it will be your undoing one of these days! Mama says so, Mama always says…"

"A pox on what Mother says," Alison replied, her voice calm but laden with venom. "I'm going to bed."

"I suppose this means you hate me too," Jennet sniffled as Alison got up to leave.

"No," her sister replied with a cursory glance over her shoulder. "I don't hate you. I do pity you, though. You didn't ask to be born into this, to be such a poor little wretch. You didn't ask to be a bastard. I sometimes think it probably would have been better for you if you'd never been born."

And with those final callous words, Alison left.

Jennet spent the rest of the evening in a daze. Half exhausted and half in shock, she stayed rooted to her spot in the corner. She watched as hour by long hour each guest ate and drank themselves further into a stupor. She looked on as her grandmother performed some of her favourite party tricks, the great aged lady clearly revelling in the gasps of her guests as she produced a piggin of butter which she had churned using magic that very evening. She listened as the volume in the room reached a riotous crescendo before beginning to dissipate as friends and neighbours either left or fell asleep wherever they lay down. For all that time she sat, thinking, her sister's words whirring around her mind, planting their seeds, injecting their poison.

A bastard. A poor little wretch. These were familiar words to Jennet; words which had long since ceased to hurt her. She had known for as long as she could remember that she was different from the rest of her family, that she was a Device in name only.

What she hadn't known, however, was how closely bound her arrival into this world was with John Device's demise. She hadn't known, or at least it had never occurred to her, that her mother had broken her siblings' father's heart, that he had ailed as a result of her mother's betrayal as well as Chattox's witchcraft. She knew that she was a child born in sin, but until tonight she had never realised just how grave that sin had been. For the first time in her life, Jennet wished that her questions hadn't been answered.

Jennet looked down into her lap, the heat of emerging tears burning behind her eyes. It was no wonder that Alison pitied her. In that moment, she pitied herself; here she was, sitting alone in a corner and not a single person had shown any concern for her. Quite clearly she was not enjoying herself; quite clearly her sister had upset her and yet, where was her mother? Her grandmother? Her brother? Too busy enjoying themselves to notice her, to talk to her, to ask her what was wrong and why was she sitting alone. It was the story of her life, she thought. She was the forgotten child, condemned to be forever neglected, resented, and pitied. Perhaps, like Alison said, it would have been better if she'd never been born.

"Jennet, what are you doing down here? Shouldn't you be in bed?" A gentle voice addressed her. She looked up to see Jennet Preston standing over her, her bright green eyes etched with curiosity and, Jennet thought, concern.

Jennet shook her head at her mother's friend, a petted lip sneaking out before she could prevent it. She felt the first of those hot tears begin to fall.

"Oh, little Jennet! What's wrong?" Jennet Preston asked her. She bent down, placing a consoling hand upon her shoulder.

Jennet looked up at her, studying her friendly, familiar face, a face she had known all of her life. She thought about what Alison had said, how she had called Jennet Preston a whore. Even the memory of the word made her shudder. She couldn't believe it was true. She couldn't believe that this kind, pretty woman was capable of anything terrible. If Master Lister had fallen in love with her then surely that was his fault, not hers.

"Overtired, no doubt," Elizabeth snapped, approaching her from the other side of the room. "You should have been in your bed hours ago. What have you been doing?"

"Just sitting here," Jennet replied, her response muted as she tried to suppress her tears. She stood up, trying her best to look indignant. "And I'm not tired. I'm not a baby. I'm ten now."

Jennet Preston gave her an amused smile. "Indeed you are, but I think your mother may have a point. It is rather late. Even your big brother has gone to bed."

"Where is your sister?" Elizabeth asked, her hands falling to their favoured spot on her hips.

"In bed," Jennet replied.

"Well then, I suggest you make your way there as well."

Jennet frowned, her lip quivering. "I don't want to sleep with Alison tonight, Mama. She was unkind to me."

Her mother rolled her eyes impatiently. "What's she done now?"

Jennet's breath caught in her throat. As upset as she was with Alison, she didn't dare to repeat all the dreadful things she had said. "She called me a bastard again," she replied, giving her mother a safe portion of the truth.

Elizabeth grimaced. "I'm sick of hearing that word from her. Just wait until I speak to her tomorrow. Now, off to bed."

"But I don't want to share with Alison," Jennet began to whine.

Elizabeth threw her hands up in despair. "Where else are you going to sleep, Jennet? Not with me! I've grown used to having a bed to myself – the relief I felt when you were old enough to go in with your sister, you used to kick me all night long…"

Jennet's face fell. "I'll sleep right here then. On the floor."

"No you won't. You can come in with me, lass." Jennet spun around to see her grandmother standing there, her expression weary and resigned but her arms outstretched and welcoming. "One night can't hurt, I suppose."

Jennet ran towards her and gave her a grateful hug. Normally she would never wish to sleep in her grandmother's bed; it had a strange smell and besides, the old woman snored loudly enough to wake the dead. But right now she couldn't care. Anything was better than sleeping next to Alison. "Thank you Grand-mama."

Demdike patted her head affectionately. "Come on, lass. We will sort out all this nonsense with Alison in the morning. Chances are she's just had too much ale and it has loosened that sharp tongue of hers. No harm done, I'm sure."

"But she was really, really unkind to me, Grand-mama," Jennet protested as they headed towards Demdike's little room.

"She's unkind to all of us," Elizabeth quipped from behind her. "That's just Alison. She says some awful things to me. She's called me all the names under the sun, you know, she…"

Demdike let out a heavy sigh, interrupting her daughter. "Just words. As I said, no harm done."

"Yes, just words," Jennet repeated. "Good night, Mama. And good night, Jennet," she added, giving her mother's friend a broad smile which was readily returned. Yes, she thought again, Jennet Preston was a nice lady. Little Bess was very lucky to have a mother like her.

Jennet took hold of her grandmother's hand, glancing up at the aged lady as she shuffled unsteadily along. Her mother hadn't been quite correct when she said that Alison was unkind to everyone. Alison harboured a lot of anger and resentment, that was true, but none of it was ever directed at her grandmother. Indeed, Alison seemed to idolise Demdike, to be in awe of her great age and experience, to be desperate to learn from her, to share her gifts and abilities. Jennet considered that perhaps if Demdike spoke to Alison about her behaviour, instead of leaving it to Elizabeth to deliver a fiery reprimand, Alison might actually listen. She opened her mouth to speak but one glance at her grandmother's exhausted face as she climbed into bed told her that the suggestion was best left until morning.

Jennet got into bed beside Demdike and pulled a blanket up and under her chin. Contrary to her earlier protestations she was tired, and immediately she closed her eyes. As her grandmother snored softly beside her she began to drift, but even in her sleepy state her mind kept wandering back towards Alison's cruel taunts. They were just words, she told herself; Grand-mama had said so. Just words, and yet…did words not have the power to harm? Is that not what she had learned time and time again over these past few years? Did she not know from experience that when her mother, her brother and her grandmother said a few choice words, they contained the power to harm or to heal? Was there ever any such thing as 'just words'?

Jennet's eyes flew open. She turned over, looking at her grandmother as she slept. Her kind, loving grandmother. The one person who never seemed to tease her, who never scolded her, who let her sneak some bread when she was hungry, who seemed to care the most. And yet, if Chattox and her family were to be believed, this old woman was no cunning woman, no healer at all, but one of the most powerful and wicked witches Pendle had ever known. Jennet stared at her, mesmerised, watching the rise and fall of her chest, listening to the rhythm of her breathing. She studied her face; her sharp features, her lines and wrinkles, the remnants of frowns, of smiles, of a lifetime of expressions and feelings etched all over her skin. She looked so ordinary, so benign. She looked nothing like a witch at all. But then, Jennet thought, neither did her mother or brother. And yet, she knew what she had seen and heard. She knew what they had said; she knew what their words had done.

Just words, indeed. There was no such thing. As Jennet settled down to sleep once more, a final, unwelcome thought crept over her: if Mama and James truly had the power to curse, it could have only been passed down by Grand-mama, by Old Demdike, the so-called devil woman. And if that was the case, what terrible deeds had Demdike committed with those same curses in her long and notorious life?

Part Two

1611 - 1612

"Barbarous and inhumane Monster, beyond example; so farre from sensible understanding of thy owne miserie, as to bring thy owne naturall children into mischiefe and bondage; and thy selfe to be a witnesse vpon the Gallowes, to see thy owne children, by thy devillish instructions hatcht up in Villanie and Witchcraft, to suffer with thee"

Thomas Potts, The Wonderfull Discoverie of Witches in the Countie of Lancaster

5

St Peter's Day 1611
'Henry Bulcock's Child'

Jennet ran up the hillside as fast as her legs could carry her, so fast that she almost felt dizzy. She had grown in recent weeks, the hemline on her skirts becoming shorter and testifying to her lengthening limbs. The height difference was subtle and she was still small for her age, but nonetheless Jennet felt pleased about it. She would be eleven in a few months' time and for some reason, she liked the idea of growing up.

Her mother, of course, had been quick to notice the change. "I think we'll need to find you another petticoat," she'd said. "I'm sure Alison will have something she can give you."

Alison had complained, of course, and no new petticoat had as yet been forthcoming. Jennet didn't mind, though. She didn't want Alison's old cast-offs anyway and besides, slightly shorter skirts made running much easier.

Ill-fitting boots, however, were another matter. Jennet groaned, her toes pressing painfully against them as she sprinted through the long grass. In the end she kicked them off, liberating her feet with a satisfied sigh. She slowed her pace then, clutching her boots in her hands and relishing the feeling of the hard, sun-scorched earth pressed against her skin as she walked the rest of the way home. It had been a hot, dry start to the summer, one of the hottest she could remember. Everyone else seemed perturbed by this, concerned at the lack of rainfall. There were mutterings about failed harvests, about ruin for the landowners and starvation for the tenants. Jennet didn't care about any of this. It wasn't like there was ever enough for her to eat anyway, even when the harvest was good. At least this way she had been able to enjoy the sunshine. Life always seemed better when the sun shone.

Jennet reached the top of the incline, the ground beneath her bare feet becoming flatter as the old stone exterior of Malkin Tower grew nearer. Weary, she slumped down, reluctantly putting her boots back on. Ill-fitting or not, her mother would not approve of her wandering around barefoot.

"What if you catch a chill?" she'd ask. "Or stand on something sharp? You'll do yourself a terrible mischief, Jennet Device. People were not made to walk around without any boots on."

Jennet shook her head at the imagined sound of one of her mother's lectures. There was no end to Elizabeth Device's sense of foreboding, especially when it came to her children. Jennet lay back on the ground, staring dreamily at the blue, cloudless sky, watching as the evening light began to paint it with hues of orange and red. She was in no hurry to walk those final few steps to Malkin Tower and go inside. It had been a wonderful day; the sort of day she would remember forever. She had spent most of it down at the river nearby, paddling in the cool, shallow waters, trying to catch small fish with her hands. It had been quiet and peaceful, with none of the other local children coming down to interrupt her game or to taunt her. In short, it had been perfect. Too perfect to end. If she stayed out here, she thought, she might just be able to prolong it a little bit longer.

Her thoughts were interrupted by a loud knocking noise, followed swiftly by raised voices. Jennet sat up, peering over the long blades of grass as she looked over towards Malkin Tower, trying to identify the source of the commotion. From this distance she could see a man, small in stature with a round belly and a prominent beard. He was standing at the door of her home, waving his arms around excitedly and having a heated discussion with Jennet's mother, who was also doing her fair share of wild gesticulation. Jennet's interest piqued. Who was this man, and what did he want? Why did he seem so angry? Unable to contain her curiosity but keen to remain unseen, Jennet shuffled forward on her belly, drawing herself nearer in the hopes that she might listen to the discussion unfold.

"Goodman Bulcock, I can assure you that my daughter is capable of no such thing," Jennet heard her mother say. Jennet gulped hard on hearing her mother's denial – which daughter did she mean?

"Oh, she is," the man insisted. "She did it – I witnessed it myself. Roaming, thieving no-good beggar that she is."

Jennet sighed with relief. A roaming beggar – that had to be Alison, not her. She rolled her eyes at the prospect of her sister being in yet more trouble. No surprises there.

Elizabeth Device smoothed her hands over her apron. "I admit my daughter is a little wayward at times," she said evenly, changing tack. "I'm sure you'll understand that it is difficult, when there is no father at home. As you'll know, my dear husband John passed away..." Elizabeth added with obvious sorrow.

Jennet was forced to suppress a giggle as that final, predictable line fell from her mother's lips. She had watched her mother do this scores of times when neighbours came knocking at the door to complain about one of her siblings' misdemeanours - a firm denial at first, followed by a plea for pity. It usually worked. Fools, her mother would call them as they went on their way, either placated or at the very least, subdued. Complete and utter fools.

This man Bulcock, however, was not to be fooled. "That might be the case, and if she hadn't done something so serious, I might have been prepared to accept that. But Goodwife Device, this is not mere mischief that your daughter has done. You must see that her actions are far graver than being a beggar and a nuisance? For heaven's sake," he shouted, his voice beginning to waver, "my child could die!"

Jennet clapped her hand over her mouth in horror. A child could die? What on earth had Alison done?

Elizabeth Device stared at him, her jaw set hard, just as it always was when she was about to lose her temper. Jennet held her breath, unable to move. "As I told you, Goodman Bulcock," she replied through gritted teeth, "Alison is not capable of such a thing."

"God's death!" he replied, placing his head in his hands. "You must think I am stupid. Christ's wounds, her grandmother is Old Demdike!"

"I'll thank you to stop taking the Lord's name in vain, Goodman," Elizabeth replied.

"Ha! This is no Godly house," he snorted. "'Tis a coven of witches. Witches – every last one of you."

Before Jennet could blink, she saw her sister run forth, falling to her knees at Goodman Bulcock's feet. "I am so sorry," she cried, hands clasped together, "I beg you, forgive me, I didn't mean it – my words were spoken only in temper. I wish I could take them back. I wish I hadn't uttered them at all."

Elizabeth Device looked at her eldest daughter, open-mouthed. "Alison, what is the meaning of this?" she asked.

Alison stared helplessly at her mother. Even from this distance Jennet could tell that she was crying, her face crumpled, her shoulders sunken and shaking. "It happened yesterday, in Barley. I was visiting a friend when I came upon a little girl – Goodman Bulcock's child – playing on the lane. The girl seemed to recognise me and began to shout taunt and jibes, calling me a beggar, a thief and a witch. I walked away but the child kept following me. I became angry and before I could stop myself I…I cursed her."

Jennet heard her mother gasp. She wrung her hands in her apron, just as she always did when she was anxious. She looked cautiously from her daughter to Goodman Bulcock who stood there, silent and expectant. "Goodman, I had no idea about any of this," she said. "I am truly sorry for my daughter's actions."

"Sorry!" Goodman Bulcock repeated, throwing his hands up in the air. "Sorry won't cure my daughter! Sorry won't release her from the clutches of her foul and heinous words! It's begun already, you know - the sickness. She is in bed as we speak, gripped by a dreadful fever, a wasting malady the like of which I have never seen before. She will surely die unless your witch of a daughter undoes her terrible work." Goodman Bulcock put his head in his hands.

Alison lurched forward. "Please, Goodman," she pleaded. "Please believe me – I don't know how to undo this. If I did, I would, but they were words spoken in anger, slipping out before I could stop them. Forgive me. Please, forgive me!" she cried, grabbing the man's arm as she cried uncontrollably.

Goodman Bulcock recoiled. "Get off me, witch," he growled.

"What is all this?" came a voice from the doorway. Jennet watched as her Grandmother shuffled forward, aided by James upon whose arm she placed a shaking hand. "Can an old woman get no peace to sleep in the evening? What is going on?"

Jennet strained to hear as her mother bent down, a grim expression on her face as she recounted the sorry tale to Old Demdike. Demdike listened intently, nodding then shaking her head at intervals, her previously sleepy eyes now wide as she absorbed everything she was being told. Jennet could hardly breathe; she was so anxious. Grand-mama will know what to do, she tried to tell herself. Grand-mama always knows what to do.

"Alison, my dear, what did you say to this man's child, exactly?" Old Demdike asked, pursing her lips as she awaited her sobbing granddaughter's response.

"The girl kept saying that I was a filthy beggar, so filthy that I made her feel sick," Alison replied, sniffling. "So I turned and I told her that if that was the case, I hoped she did become ill; I wished that she would waste away and die so that I didn't have to listen to her vile little tongue any longer."

Jennet saw her mother flinch as Alison repeated her dreadful words. Old Demdike gave her granddaughter a stern look. "I thought I'd taught you better than that, lass. You were careless with your words and you were very unkind, although," she added, moving her severe gaze to Goodman Bulcock, "I could say the same about your daughter. It's Henry Bulcock, isn't it? Your family have a smallholding out near Barley, don't they? If my old memory serves me my late husband knew your father very well."

Goodman Bulcock nodded awkwardly in response. "Yes, that's right," he confirmed.

From her grassy hiding place, Jennet couldn't help but smile. Grand-mama knew everybody around these parts. And what's more, she knew everything about them, too.

"Alison hasn't cursed your child, Goodman Bulcock," Old Demdike continued. "She cannot curse her because she doesn't know how. She has, however, ill-wished her. But these were mere words uttered in a fit of temper; just words which could have been said by anyone. I can assure you, they have no power over your daughter."

Jennet frowned. This was different to what she had been told. She had always believed that ill-wishing was witchcraft, that words spoken in such a way did have the power to harm. She had seen the price of ill-wishing, too, she thought with a shudder, recalling her own mother's malicious words and the subsequent deaths of the Robinson brothers. Now her Grandmother was telling this man that ill-wishing didn't mean anything, that words spoken in this way held no power at all. How could that possibly be true?

Goodman Bulcock didn't seem convinced either. "But those words were not spoken by anyone; they were spoken by the granddaughter of Old Demdike. Everyone knows what you and your family are capable of! Of course her accursed tongue was effective - my child is sick, she is dying at home in her bed and it is because of your girl. I ought to go to the constable about the lot of you!"

At the mention of the law, Jennet's mother leapt forward, grabbing Henry Bulcock by the hand. "Please, Goodman, I beg you not to involve the constable! I beg you, for my children's sake…"

"Let me go, hideous woman!" Goodman Bulcock cried, shaking her off.

"Don't you talk to my mother like that!" James shouted, stepping forward, his considerable tall, thin frame looming threateningly over their angry visitor. Bulcock, however, seemed to hold his ground, returning James's furious glare with equal venom.

Jennet stared, unable to look away, her breathing growing rapid as the scene before her fell apart. This was bad, very bad. This was getting out of control. This could spell ruin for them all.

In the midst of the descending chaos, only Old Demdike seemed to remain calm. "Do you intend to go to the constable, Goodman Bulcock? Because if you do, I must ask you to leave. My family and I will answer no more of your questions. Go home – go back to your wife and your poorly child and leave us in peace."

Henry Bulcock gave a resigned sigh. "No," he admitted. "I will not go to the constable. I fear what you would do to me if I did. And besides, the constable can't cure my girl of this affliction. Frankly, I cannot see the point."

Demdike gave a small smile. "I'm glad that you will not involve the law in this. We are, as you see, simple and innocent people. We will, of course, pray for your daughter's recovery from this awful malady. And," she added, labouring her words, "if there is anything else we can do to help, please just ask. We are good neighbours; just ask anyone around these parts."

Henry Bulcock gave a grim smile, glancing at the ground as he considered his next words. "Goodwife Southerns," he said, addressing Jennet's grandmother by her proper name for the first time, "many say that you are a skilled and capable healer. Would you consider coming to my home and taking a look at the girl? It may be that you know of some remedy to ease her suffering and bring her back to health. I would pay you in kind, of course."

Old Demdike put up a hand in protest, flashing him a yellow grin. "No need for payment – call it a gesture of the goodwill between our two families. I will come at once." She turned to her grandson. "James, please fetch my shawl and my case of remedies. You will accompany me. My eyes and legs are not what they were."

And with that, disaster was averted. Jennet watched as her grandmother went slowly down the hill, flanked on either side by James and Henry Bulcock. She stretched out on her grassy spot, feeling the tension of the last few minutes leave her weary, aching limbs. Grand-mama never ceased to amaze her; she always knew exactly what to do. She could cure and she could heal, but she could understand people too; she could predict what they might say and what they might do and then use that to turn them towards her way of thinking. There was no doubt about it, her grandmother had magical abilities. In fact, Jennet thought as she finally stood up to go inside, after what she had seen today, she believed that her grandmother could work miracles.

It was the following morning before Old Demdike and James finally returned to Malkin Tower. After a restless night beside Alison, Jennet had woken early to the sound of the first rain they'd had for weeks as it poured into every vulnerable crack that their old cottage had to offer. She had lain in bed for some time, listening to Alison's soft snores as they competed with the relentless drip, drip, drip of the water until, annoyed by the prospect of a day stuck indoors, she had got up and gone to find her grandmother. With the tedium of a rainy day stretched in front of her, she was desperate for some amusement and couldn't wait to hear Grand-mama's tales of last night's adventure. However, when she opened her grandmother's door she found her room to be cold, her blankets folded and clearly unused. Furrowing her little brow, Jennet went to find her mother.

"Where is Grand-mama?" she'd asked a flustered-looking Elizabeth Device as she rattled around in front of the hearth, trying to create a pottage from sparse ingredients.

Her mother spun around, her hands immediately finding their way to her hips. "She's not returned home yet, why?"

"I wanted to know how her visit to the Bulcock's home went,"

Jennet replied. She shot her mother an earnest glance, her eyes quickly darting to the pot which was warming on the hearth. Her stomach growled.

Jennet's mother followed her gaze. "Pottage isn't ready yet. It's very thin and we've no bread, so don't go getting your hopes up. You'll be lucky to get supper today, never mind anything else. Anyway," she added, "what do you know about Grand-mama's visit to the Bulcocks?"

Jennet swallowed hard, her mouth salivating at the prospect of even a watery meal. When she'd got home last night there had been no supper, no welcome, just a quiet, sullen house. She'd gone straight to bed, falling asleep before the sun had even set. Another reason for waking so early, she thought. "I heard you all talking," she replied, trying her best to sound casual. "I was playing a bit further down the hill. You were all talking very loudly, you know," she added pointedly.

"Aye, you were eavesdropping more like," her mother retorted, turning back to the hearth. "Well, you know the whole sorry story then. I just hope your grandmother can heal the little wretch and we will hear no more about this."

"Do you think Alison did hurt that little girl?" Jennet asked. "Do you think what she said made her sick?"

"Like Grand-mama said, Alison couldn't have done it," Elizabeth replied as she stirred the pottage. She didn't turn around and Jennet couldn't see her expression, but there was something about the tone of her voice that was less than convincing.

Before Jennet could ask anything more, a damp gust of air blew in as the door swung open and Old Demdike hobbled inside, escorted by James who hovered protectively over the old woman as though she might break at any moment. Seeing the state of her mother Elizabeth gasped, grabbing a wooden stool and bringing it to her.

"Sit, Mother, sit," she insisted. "You're too old and frail for all of this."

Old Demdike waved a dismissive hand. "Nonsense! Your boy

looked after me; strapping young lad that he is. And we only walked part of the way home; Goodman Bulcock was kind enough to bring us along the lane in his cart. Mind you," she added, rubbing the bottom of her back, "I think I'd have been better walking."

Elizabeth clicked her tongue disapprovingly. "What a carry-on," she observed, shaking her head. "So, did you cure the child?"

"Of course, lass," Old Demdike replied, flashing Jennet a small smile. Jennet beamed back at her. If there was one thing which her grandmother took pride in above all else, it was her healing abilities. "Jennet, be an angel and fetch your old Grand-mama a jug of small ale. You may have the bit off the top."

"Thank you, Grand-mama," Jennet replied, licking her dry lips. In truth she was thirsty; she had taken a few sips of the cool stream waters whilst playing yesterday but had drunk very little since.

"You spoil that child," Elizabeth snapped, wiping her hands on her apron.

This time it was Old Demdike's turn to click her tongue. "Even little lasses like our Jennet need a drink in the morning," she retorted with a grateful nod as Jennet returned with the ale, taking the few gulps she was allowed.

"Grand-mama, can you tell us how you cured the girl?" Jennet asked, unable to wait any longer to hear the delicious details.

Elizabeth gave an exasperated sigh. "You've a head full of nonsense, Jennet Device. Stories and nonsense that are no use to anyone."

"It took all night," Old Demdike began, ignoring her daughter's lecture. "The child had a terrible fever and was in the grip of some mighty convulsions. But, thanks to a few carefully chosen remedies and a good deal of cool water from the stream, the fever broke at dawn. She will need to rest for a few days, but I believe she is out of danger now. And speaking of rest," she added, draining the last drop of ale in her jug, "I haven't slept all night. I am going to bed." The old woman heaved herself off her stool and began to walk towards the door. "Be a good girl for your mother now, little one," she said. "Don't get under her feet."

"I won't," Jennet promised. "I'm so glad you cured the girl. Do you know what caused her illness?"

Old Demdike shrugged. "Could be any number of things," she replied. "The main thing is that she will be well again."

"Could it have been what Alison said?" The words tumbled from Jennet's lips before she could stop them.

"Jennet! I've already told you…" Elizabeth began, swiping a hand towards her daughter. Jennet ducked swiftly away from her mother's reach.

Old Demdike turned back around, a small frown forming on her aged brow. "That is a dangerous thing to keep saying, lass. If you don't want any more trouble in this house, I'd thank you not to say it again."

"So it wasn't Alison?" Jennet persisted.

"No, it wasn't," Old Demdike replied as she turned away.

Jennet stared after her as the old woman limped tentatively towards her room, leaning heavily on her rickety wooden stick. Her grandmother was adamant that none of this had anything to do with Alison; she had been certain yesterday when speaking to Henry Bulcock, and she was certain now, even after curing the girl of her mysterious illness. But if Alison's words weren't the cause, then what was? Jennet thought again about the other deaths which had occurred after words spoken by her family. John Robinson, James Robinson and John Duckworth had all been ill-wished and with them the awful words had worked; why were Alison's words any different?

Perhaps they weren't any different. As Old Demdike closed her door, an awful thought occurred to Jennet, a thought which had never occurred to her before. Was her grandmother lying to her? Jennet felt dizzy, her head spinning as the devastating possibility dawned. She slumped down against the cold stone wall. If Grandmama had lied it was surely to protect her family, to keep trouble away from their door. These were noble, good intentions of course, but a lie was still a lie and lies, Jennet knew, always came at a price.

Slowly, with all the courage she could muster, Jennet counted out the names she knew, the victims of her family's malice. John Robinson, James Robinson, John Duckworth, Mistress Towneley and now Henry Bulcock's child, who had been saved only by Old Demdike's intervention. Five people, and those were just the ones she knew about. How many more were there? And more importantly, she thought, how many more people would be harmed by the Devices and their foul tempers, their deadly words and deeds?

6

**Autumn 1611
'Whores and Witches'**

Jennet wandered along the lane, listening to the sound of the mud as it squelched underfoot. Every so often she would bury her boots deeper into it, pressing them down hard and enjoying the soft, satisfying feeling of the dirt as it receded beneath her. She knew her mother would chastise her for the state of her boots, but she didn't care. After all, her mother was always cross about something, and at the moment she was crosser than ever – that was part of the reason why Jennet was out by herself, idling along the lane in the first place. Besides, she liked the way it felt. She liked that each time she did it, she would win and the mud would yield. As strange and ridiculous as the game was, she liked the feeling that, even for the briefest second, she had control over something.

Autumn had arrived early this year, bringing heavy rains which soaked the fields and turned the falling leaves to brown mush. There had been little colour; those delightful oranges, red and yellows had been a rarity which she had struggled to find, much to her frustration. Normally she would collect those colourful leaves, taking them back home and hiding them under her bed. Sometimes, when Alison wasn't around to tease her, she would take them out and examine them, admire them for the things of beauty that they were. She would do this over and over again until they withered and crumbled and could be looked upon no more. This autumn had brought her no such joy, the changing season marked only by lanes filled with pathetic brown foliage, shrivelled up and pressed miserably into the growing bog. So, she thought, she would just have to occupy herself with the mud.

"Jennet Device is covered in lice!" a mocking voice called from behind her.

Jennet stopped in her tracks, trying to decide if she should turn around. She recognised the voice as one of the boys from the nearby village; one of the usual suspects who habitually taunted her whenever their paths crossed. Although he was a couple of years older than her, he was a skinny, cowardly specimen who only ever dared to pick on her when she was on her own. She didn't know his name, nor was she interested to find out; she just wished he would leave her in peace. After a moment's thought she decided to walk on, to ignore his silly rhymes and mockery and to continue her journey home. If she didn't answer him, if she didn't rise to his bait, then perhaps he would give up and leave her alone.

"Jennet Device reeks of dead mice!"

The jibe was met by a chorus of laughter which caused Jennet to jolt. Clearly, the boy wasn't alone. She continued on, raising her petticoat a little with her fingers so that she could walk a bit faster. Inwardly she cursed Alison for finally giving in and relinquishing a fresh hand-me-down. It had been so much easier to run with her old one. Still, she thought, it could be worse. At least today the boys were content to mock her. Usually they would have caught up with her by now, shoving her and leaving her face down in the mud.

"My father says your mother's a whore and you're a bastard!" the boy called.

"Aye, and your sister, too. My big brother says she does it for food," another boy chipped in. "Does your Mama not feed any of you?" he mocked.

"She mustn't – look at Jennet, the skinny little runt. I bet you stink of mice because you have to eat them!" the first boy yelled.

His joke was greeted with laughter and more chants and rhymes. Jennet marched on, clenching her fists. She tried her best to look as though she didn't care what they said or what they did to her. But inside, her heart was bursting and tears pricked behind her eyes. It was hard not to feel upset. After all, what had she ever done to them? She had been walking along the lane, squelching the mud, lost in her own little world as usual. She hadn't done anything wrong. She hadn't asked for any of this. Behind her she could hear their footsteps grow closer as they caught up, her tiny strides no match for theirs. Inwardly she sighed, looking down at the sodden, sticky ground. She had enjoyed the mud before. Now she wished it wasn't there.

"If you're going to push me over, can't you just get it over with?" she said, finally turning around to face them. Her heart sank as she saw that today there were three of them. Three versus one wasn't a fair fight at all. Whatever they were planning to do, she hoped they would make it quick.

The first boy feigned surprise. "Why on earth would we do that, little Jennet?" he asked. "We just wanted to talk to you."

"About what?" Jennet eyed them suspiciously.

"We wanted to ask you a question."

"That's right," the second boy added. "We heard a rumour about your sister and we want to know if it's true."

Jennet shrugged. "There's always a new rumour about Alison."

The boys sniggered. "Aye but this one's a bit different to all of the others," one of them said. "There's talk that your sister has been following in your grandmother's footsteps, that your grandmother is teaching her to become a witch."

"Grand-mama isn't a witch," Jennet replied. "She's a healer. She helps people."

"Aye, sometimes she does," the boy replied. "Henry Bulcock's been telling folk that she healed his girl."

"Yes, that's right," Jennet said, triumphant. "As I said, Grand-mama can heal people."

"But Henry Bulcock also said that it was your sister who made his daughter sick in the first place. She placed a curse on her, a curse which only your grandmother knew how to lift. Is that true, Jennet?"

Jennet shook her head slightly, looking at the three faces before her, their expressions half-inquisitive, half-sneering. She remembered her grandmother's words to her on that day, how she had warned her that it was dangerous to speak of these things. Standing before these nasty, rumour-mongering boys now, it began to dawn on her just how dangerous it was. "It's true that Grandmama healed her," she began, "but…"

"But how did she know how to lift the curse?" one of the boys asked, interrupting her. "My mother says she could only know how to lift curses if she knows how to make them as well."

"Aye that's right," another boy added. "There's a reason she's known as Old Demdike, isn't there? She's a witch."

"And your sister is a witch, too," the first boy declared, giving Jennet a shove which caused her to stumble backwards. "So, are you a witch as well, then?"

"No way!" one of the other boys answered. "Look at her, she's a pathetic little bastard. There's no way she's got any powers."

Before Jennet could draw breath the boys set upon her, pushing and shoving her so hard that she soon found herself on the ground. As she sat in the mud they circled her, continuing to chant and mock. She looked up at them, feeling dizzy and panicked, but also resigned. This was how it always went; she knew that if she just sat there, if she let them have their fun, they would soon get bored and move on. After all, what else could she do? She could hardly retaliate; she had neither the words nor the physical presence to overcome them. In that respect, they were right about her: she had no power, no power at all.

"Edward! Richard! Simon! What mischief is this? What have you done to my granddaughter?"

The boys fell silent and turned around. Though their legs

partially obscured her view, Jennet could see her grandmother standing unsteadily on the soft, uneven surface, supported by Alison who was giving the boys a hard glare.

"Well," Alison said, "I believe my grandmother asked you a question. Why is my sister on the ground?" Alison glanced down at Jennet, giving her that look which Jennet always hated, the one which spoke of her pity and disappointment in equal measure.

"Erm, I...we..." one of the boys stammered. "We were just playing, just teasing her a little." He glanced down at Jennet and she saw that his face had turned a perfect shade of scarlet. "I'm really very sorry, Old D- I mean, Goodwife Southerns. We meant no harm," he added, stepping away from her as though to distance himself from his guilt.

"Is this true, little one?" Old Demdike asked, her voice tender.

Slowly, Jennet pulled herself up on to her feet, dusting herself down in a futile effort to clean off some of the mud which clung to her clothing. She walked over to her grandmother, cementing herself by her side as she laid her best pair of wide, innocent eyes upon the three scarlet, shamed faces in front of her. They had been torturing her for as long as she could remember and she had been defenceless against them. But not anymore. Today they had picked on her for the last time; she would make sure of that.

"No Grand-mama," she replied, allowing a little sob to escape from her lips. In truth she was past feeling upset, but she knew that a few tears wouldn't hurt her cause. Beside her, she sensed Alison roll her eyes. "We were not playing. They were frightening me. They always frighten me. I thought they were going to hurt me."

Jennet's terrified words were all the ammunition that Old Demdike needed. The old woman straightened her crumpled spine, drawing herself up as high as she could to look them squarely in the eye. As small and frail as she was, there was something formidable about her grandmother when she was angry. "How dare you," she said, poking each of them in the chest with her walking stick. "How dare you hurt my granddaughter! Mark my words, if I ever see any of you anywhere near her again, you will all pay a heavy price. Now, go!"

The boys didn't need to be told twice. They sped off, swiftly departing from the lane and into one of the fields to make a quick escape.

"That's right!" Alison cried after them, shaking her fists. "You'll have me to deal with, too!"

"That's enough, Alison," Old Demdike cautioned. She gave a weary sigh and leaned heavily on her stick, wrapping her other arm around her youngest granddaughter. "Are you alright now, little one?"

Jennet nodded gratefully. "I'm so glad you came," she replied. "I hope they leave me alone now."

"Aye lass, me too. What are you doing all the way down here, anyway? Does your mother know where you are?"

Jennet shook her head slightly, avoiding her grandmother's disapproving gaze. She didn't want to admit that she was out here to avoid her mother's bad temper, or that this lane wasn't half as far as she had strayed across the country which surrounded Malkin Tower. She loved Grand-mama; the last thing she wanted to do was worry her, to let her think that she was following in Alison's roaming footsteps. "What will you do to them if they don't leave me alone, Grand-mama?" Jennet asked, quickly changing the subject.

"Speak to their parents. I know all three families well; I doubt they'd be happy to hear what their wayward sons had been up to," Old Demdike replied.

"Oh," said Jennet, unable to hide her disappointment.

Her grandmother gave her a curious smile. "Why, what were you hoping for?"

"I don't know…perhaps you could do a spell or something?"

"Oh for goodness sake, Jennet," Alison began with a sigh.

"No, let the lass speak," Old Demdike insisted, silencing Alison with a wave of her hand. "What sort of spell would you like me to do for you, lass?" she asked.

Jennet let out a delighted giggle. She was unaccustomed to

being indulged in this way. "I don't know – something annoying, something which would really upset them like they upset me." She closed her eyes for a moment, trying to rein in her racing imagination. "If I had the power, I'd make frogs come out of their mouths whenever they spoke!"

Old Demdike laughed. "Well, as you know, little one, I ply a trade as a healer. But, having said that, I think that is an excellent idea. Although I'd make one suggestion – I'd conjure some toads rather than frogs."

"Oh. Why?" Jennet asked, furrowing her brow.

"Because those boys have been little toads towards you," her grandmother replied with a snort.

"Oh, Grandmother!" Alison threw up her arms in despair. "Don't encourage her! Don't you think you've done enough for one day?"

Old Demdike's smile faded. "Aye, perhaps. But nasty little toads often turn into nasty big toads when they grow up. Let that be a lesson for you, Jennet; a lesson which Alison and I know only too well," she added with a small sigh.

"Aye," replied Alison, lifting her skirts over the thick mud as they began to walk again. She glanced grimly at Jennet and her grandmother. "Speaking of which, time to go home and give mother the bad news."

"The bad news about what?" Jennet asked, taking her grandmother's arm.

"We've been to see Richard Baldwin," Alison replied, glancing cautiously at Old Demdike. "I think it's fair to say that there will be no work for Mother at the mill anymore."

Elizabeth Device did not receive her mother and daughter's news well. Jennet spent the rest of the afternoon sat outside the kitchen door, tucked up in her favourite corner, listening to what was being said. Upon arriving home, it was made clear to her that she should make herself scarce. She didn't need to be told twice: she knew from experience that the only thing worse than an altercation between her mother and Alison was one between her mother and grandmother. A heated discussion between all three of them just didn't bear thinking about.

"That Baldwin is a rotten man," Old Demdike said. "I don't know how you managed to work for him for so long."

"Aye!" replied Elizabeth, exasperated. "I could have told you that! If I'd known what you were planning, I'd have told you not to go. Baldwin is a rogue – you were never going to get anything good from the likes of him."

"I see that now," Demdike conceded. "But we had to try, lass. He owes you the rest of your wages. Sending you home and telling you there's no more work for you is bad enough, but sending you home without giving you what you're due is worse. Someone had to fight your corner."

"And I suppose you two thought you were the ones who should do it." Jennet could sense her mother pointing a severe finger at them both. She shuddered, wrapping her arms around herself as she sought both warmth and comfort. She couldn't bear it when her mother and grandmother were at loggerheads like this.

"Who else was going to do it? You've no husband to protect you, Elizabeth. I know what that's like, lass. I know what it's like to be a woman on your own…"

"I do fine on my own."

"I know that, lass. I'm just saying, sometimes having a man in the house is useful," Demdike replied, her tone guarded. Jennet's mother always grew very defensive when it came to her lack of a husband.

"I suppose we could have asked James to go," Alison interjected. Jennet couldn't tell whether her sister was trying to be helpful or merely thinking aloud.

"James!" Elizabeth scoffed. "No – no, that would have been a bigger disaster than the pair of you going to see him. So, I presume it goes without saying then, Baldwin refused to give me what I'm owed? After all that, I'm still without work and penniless."

"Not penniless, lass. We still have the wage that James brings in and, meagre though it is, we will manage. We always do," Demdike reminded her. "But yes, Master Baldwin did refuse. In fact, he did not have a kind word for either of us."

"Oh?" Elizabeth asked.

"That's right, mother," Alison added. "He called you a whore and said Grandmother and I were witches! He threatened to burn one of us and hang the other one if we didn't get off his land." Jennet flinched at the way Alison emphasised her words. At times she hated the way her sister seemed to thrive on the most horrid gossip.

"Never mind all that," Demdike replied, her voice weary and dismissive. "What's done is done."

"Aye your grandmother is right," Elizabeth agreed. "Baldwin's not the first man to call me a whore and I daresay he won't be the last."

"But…what he said about us being witches…" Alison began, her voice faltering. Something about her muted tone caught Jennet's attention. She moved closer to the door, her ear hovering against it as she tried her best to listen.

"What about it?" Elizabeth asked.

"Grandmother, don't you think we should tell Mother what you did? What you said to Master Baldwin?"

"If you wish," Demdike replied. "Although I daresay no good will come of it. You know how your mother gets about these matters."

"We were about to leave," Alison continued, "when Grandmother turned back to Master Baldwin and said 'revenge upon him or his'. She was looking sideways as though she was talking to someone; someone who wasn't there. I'm sorry, Grandmother but I think Mother needs to know. It was really, well, shocking."

For a moment there was a heavy silence. Instinctively Jennet held her breath, too stunned to move, too stunned to exhale, her mind whirring with the details of what she had just heard.

"You cursed him?" Elizabeth asked, incredulous. "What on

Christ's wounds were you thinking, Mother? You can't go about cursing folk, you of all people know that! Look at Chattox, look at the things she does…all these years you've spent healing folk, undoing her evil deeds and now you go and curse a man! Did Baldwin hear you? Oh God - what if he goes to the sheriff? You could hang, we could all hang!"

"I know," said Demdike quietly. "In truth, I don't know if Baldwin heard me or not. I'm sorry lass; I lost my temper and for a moment I couldn't stop myself. I saw Tibb and he…"

"You saw Tibb?" Elizabeth repeated. "Oh, Lord in Heaven above!"

Jennet pressed her ear so hard against the door that it began to hurt. Her mother sounded frantic. Who was Tibb? And what had he done?

"Who's Tibb? Is that who you were talking to?" Alison asked.

Demdike let out a heavy sigh. "Tibb is a sort of spirit, lass. I've only ever seen him a couple of times before today - the first time he appeared as a young man when I was down at a stone pit near Goldshey, and the second time, a few years later when you were just a little lass, he came to me in the form of a dog. That time he made me very ill; very ill indeed."

"He made you go mad, Mother," Elizabeth interrupted, her tone sharp.

Demdike drew a deep breath. "Aye, he did. Tibb tells me things…shows me things; things which I don't often understand and which aren't always very pleasant. As I say, I hadn't seen him for years…well, until today, that is. But he once told me that he would help me from time to time, that I need only instruct him. Well, today I did. Before I could stop myself, I told him to exact revenge on that scoundrel Baldwin. I'm sorry," she said again. "I don't know what came over me. When Tibb appears it's like I'm not myself anymore – like I have no control over myself whatsoever."

"Oh, Mother!" Elizabeth exclaimed. "What are we going to do?"

The Pendle Witch Girl

"Nothing, lass," replied Demdike grimly. "Hope that Baldwin didn't hear me, I suppose. And hope that Tibb is not true to his word. As much as I want revenge, I don't wish to hang for it."

The room fell into a sombre silence as Jennet backed away from the door, shocked by what she had just heard. For a few minutes she simply stood there, frozen to the spot. She didn't know where to go or what to do; she didn't know what to think. First her mother, then James and now her beloved grandmother – all of them had been seduced by witchcraft. It was horrifying; utterly horrifying.

Jennet wandered into her bedroom, her mind still running over the details. Her grandmother had mentioned a spirit called Tibb, how he appeared and sought instructions from her, how he tempted her into committing an evil deed. James had once said the same about Dandy; he had told her how the dog would speak to him, filling his head with ideas. James had also said that when Dandy spoke to him it made him feel as though he had no control; a sentiment which her grandmother had echoed about Tibb today. Jennet gasped, recalling how James was convinced that Dandy was actually the Devil, speaking to him and instructing him. If this was true, did that mean that Tibb was in fact the Devil, too?

Jennet threw herself down on her bed in despair. She was still young and she knew that there was much about the world that she did not understand. But she knew right from wrong. Undoing witchcraft was right; healing was right, and up until today she had idolised her grandmother for her powerful, selfless work. Uttering curses, making clay pictures, and communing with the Devil through spirits and animals – those things were wrong; those things were witchcraft and today, her grandmother had crossed the line from wise woman to witch.

Jennet curled up, pressing herself into her worn blankets as she tried futilely to find some comfort. She had once wondered about her grandmother's nickname – Old Demdike, the devil woman. She had wondered if there was any truth in it; if her grandmother had earned such a reputation in earnest or if it was just another one of the many cruel rumours and accusations which surrounded her family. Well, she didn't have to wonder anymore. She closed her eyes as a solitary tear slid down her cheek. There was nothing she could do now other than face the awful truth: her grandmother was the devil woman, and she was the child of witches.

7

Spring 1612
'The Lame Pedlar'

Jennet tiptoed into the kitchen and peered around the doorway, before laughing as she reminded herself that there was no need to creep around. For the first time everyone was out: her brother and sister had disappeared at first light, while her grandmother had been called upon to help a woman in the village whose baby was on the way. Her mother had had to accompany her, of course; Grand-mama was too frail to go anywhere alone nowadays and her sight was so poor that Elizabeth Device was now effectively her eyes, especially when it came to the tricky business of delivering babies of the human or animal variety.

"She's too old for all of this," Elizabeth had muttered this morning as she hurriedly gathered up her mother's remedies.

"Shall I come with you, Mama?" Jennet had asked.

Elizabeth Device gave a sharp shake of her head. "No, you'll only be under our feet. You can stay here."

"What, alone?"

"Yes, yes, child – alone!" her mother had snapped. "You'll be twelve in the autumn – you're old enough to look after yourself for a while. And it's not like you haven't started wandering far and wide when you're playing outside anyway, is it?" she had added with a small, knowing smile. "Your grandmother told me about the day she found you down on the lane, surrounded by those boys."

Jennet had felt her face colour at the recollection. Her mother always had a knack of making her feel ashamed, even for something which absolutely had not been her fault. Of course, she wasn't given the opportunity to reply. With a final, long sigh and a customary slam of the door, her mother and grandmother had gone, leaving Jennet to fend for herself before she had the chance to decide which emotion she felt more keenly at the prospect of being home alone – delight or terror. She had sat behind that slammed door for some time after that, weighing up the situation, confronting the stillness of her home for the first time as she grappled with a sense of being simultaneously freed and abandoned. Then the first of the hunger pangs had hit her, quickly overtaking her feeling of uneasy liberation with the urge to hunt for food.

Jennet roamed around the kitchen, keeping her footsteps light as force of habit dictated. The smell of yesterday's pottage hung in the air, stale but tempting nonetheless. Jennet breathed in a little deeper than usual, prompting her stomach to protest loudly. She winced as the impatient growl echoed in the empty silence of Malkin Tower. It was a good job that she was home on her own, she thought; her stealthy footsteps were futile when they could be so easily betrayed by a rumbling belly.

Jennet crept towards the hearth and began a delicate hunt for leftovers. She looked in every possible nook and cranny but was careful to ensure that she left every pot exactly as she had found it. Past experience had taught her to be cautious. Her mother was an expert at spying a piggin or bowl out of place and would never hesitate to point an accusing finger at her youngest child.

"You're a thief, Jennet Device," she'd always say, "a wretched little thief. Mark my words, those nimble fingers will see you dangling from the end of a rope one day."

Jennet would usually skulk off to her room then, suitably

chastised and furious in equal measure. Her mother meant to warn her, of course, to discourage her from taking food whenever she pleased. The problem, Jennet thought, was that her mother's logic was flawed. Taking food from the kitchen couldn't possibly be stealing. Stealing was something you did when you took things which didn't belong to you, but the food in her house was her family's food, and therefore hers as well. It wasn't possible to steal something which was already yours. And besides, Jennet concluded, she took the food out of necessity. Otherwise, goodness knows when she'd get fed. With James and Alison and Grand-mama in the house, she was always last in line for a meal.

Jennet celebrated inwardly as she found a crust of bread, wrapped in cloth and stowed away behind a large pot. Delighted, she grabbed it and took a first, satisfying bite. It was a little dry, but she didn't mind. Beggars couldn't be choosers and besides, it tasted like victory. The bread wasn't meant for her but sheer perseverance had meant that she'd found it anyway; it was a small success, but one which she relished. For once, little Jennet Device had won – she had beaten hunger, beaten her mother's ingenious hiding places, beaten the rules. Most importantly, she had beaten the strange feeling of being alone at home and the confusing emotions which accompanied it – a chronic mixture of relief that her bewitching, cursing, devil-worshipping family had temporarily left her, combined with the more typical melancholy which assured her that not a single one of them cared what she did or how she fared.

Jennet took another keen bite, chewing hard. She knew this respite couldn't last, of course; she knew that just like her hunger those awful thoughts would return, accompanied by the heavy-hearted pangs which tied her stomach in knots. But right now there was bread to fill the hole where her anxiety and horror normally lived. She had so little to feel glad about these days that she was determined to revel in this snatched, forbidden meal. It was a triumph, and not even the dry feeling the old bread left in her mouth could take that away from her.

Jennet slumped down on to a stool, her shoulders hunched over as she teased the bread apart with her fingers. She was determined to make it last – all of it: the bread, the silence, the peace, the time alone without any conversations to overhear, any muttered words to fret over. Over the past few months she had tried her best to distance herself from it all, to stop listening outside doors, to close her ears to the gossip which seemed increasingly to surround and to consume her family. She tried not to hear the latest tale about Chattox, about Bessie Whittle, about Tibb or Dandy or pictures made from clay. She tried to close her ears as the whispers about James's involvement with Mistress Towneley's death grew louder. She tried her best to pretend not to hear that Richard Baldwin's daughter was dead, to pretend that neither this news nor the accompanying rumours of curses and bewitchment had reached her. She tried to ignore her grandmother's indignant howls when she discovered that Henry Bulcock had not only accused Alison of bewitching his daughter, but had claimed that Demdike had refused to treat her.

"It's a lie! A lie!" Grand-mama had yelled.

Jennet had put her fingers in her ears and had tried to keep them there ever since. For the first time in her life, she did not want to know; she did not want to think about what her family had done. Jennet took a final mouthful of bread, swallowing hard. She wished more than anything that she could un-see, that she could un-hear it all. She wished she could live in perfect ignorance. Sometimes, she considered, she wished that she could live without them and their awful deeds altogether. Then her dread and her fear and her terminal worry might vanish. Then she might be able to find some real peace.

As it happened, what little respite she had managed to find that afternoon was shattered by the abrupt squeal of the door as it opened into Malkin Tower. Jennet flinched as she heard her mother and grandmother make their way inside, muttering almost inaudibly to each other. Her eyes shifted immediately back towards the spot where she had found the bread, checking she had left nothing out of place. Adjusting the position of one of the pots, she listened to her mother's voice as it grew nearer. She sounded strained, upset and a little frantic. Jennet let out a heavy sigh and sat down, trying not to contemplate what might have happened now. Each day seemed to bring a new problem, a new trauma, a new piece of gossip or incident which could be endlessly discussed and debated. It was exhausting. Even if Jennet wished to keep up with it all, she knew she'd never be able to. Better not to listen at all, she thought once again.

Outside the door the voices grew louder still. "Christ's wounds! I'm at the end of my tether!" she heard her mother declare.

Jennet put her hands over her ears and rested her chin on the table. Her mother was always at her wits' end. Screwing up her eyes, she tried to remember the last time she had seen her mother look happy. Truly happy - not the sort of giddiness which possessed her when she drank too much ale, or the false smile she'd plaster on her face in front of her friends but genuine happiness, the sort which found Jennet on hot, lazy summer afternoons by the river or on crisp autumn days spent collecting colourful leaves. Even thinking about those moments made Jennet's face twitch with the urge to smile, the sort of smile which grew slowly on her face but which became so broad it made her cheeks ache. She grimaced as she realised that she had never seen her mother look this way. She had never seen that sort of sparkle in her mother's eyes; she had never seen a smile of utter delight spread itself across her lips. For as long as she could remember her mother had been worried, frazzled and short-tempered. If she was really honest with herself, for as long as she could remember her mother had been miserable.

Jennet jolted as the kitchen door burst open and her mother came bustling in, followed closely by her grandmother who hobbled cautiously behind her. Instinctively Jennet jumped up and brought her grandmother a stool. Her legs were worsening all the time, almost at the same rate as her eyesight. The old woman smiled appreciatively as Jennet pondered not for the first time the irony that such a powerful witch could have become so physically weak and decrepit.

"You need to calm yourself down, lass," Old Demdike said, trying to soothe her daughter. "Getting upset won't do any good."

"I just can't believe it, Mother! For Jennet, of all people, to be accused of witchcraft and taken away like that! It's just dreadful! After everything she has been through over the past few years…" Elizabeth's voice trailed off as she put her head in her hands and wept.

Seeing her mother's tears, Jennet's interest piqued. There was only one other Jennet aside from herself that she knew, and certainly only one Jennet in the whole world whose misfortune could provoke such distress in her mother. Jennet Preston was Elizabeth's closest and most beloved friend. Sometimes Jennet thought that her mother cared for that woman above even her own children. In fact, if she was honest with herself, she was convinced that she did. "What's happened, Grand-mama?" Jennet whispered, sitting down beside her.

"Jennet Preston has been arrested," Old Demdike replied, her voice uncharacteristically sombre. "She's been accused of witchcraft and taken away."

Jennet's eyes widened as she absorbed this news. A hundred questions swept like the wind through her mind. "Jennet Preston? Witchcraft? Who has accused her? And where have they taken her?"

"We don't know, little one. We don't know where she is. Apparently a man named Dodgson accused her of bewitching his infant son. The little boy died and this man seems to think poor Jennet had a hand in it." Old Demdike shook her head in disbelief.

"But Grand-mama," Jennet replied slowly, still trying to absorb all this information, "Jennet Preston isn't a witch, is she?"

"Of course she's not a witch, stupid girl!" Elizabeth snapped, looking up at her. Jennet gulped hard as she watched her mother's tears evaporate into fury.

"Now, now, Elizabeth, there's no need to speak to Jennet like that. She's only a child and she has questions. We all have questions about this."

"Yes, you're right. I'm sorry, Mother," Elizabeth replied. Jennet tried not to bristle at the fact that her mother did not extend the apology to her.

"As I said on the way home, lass, we need to find out what all this is about," Old Demdike said, patting Elizabeth tenderly on the hand. "There must be more to this story than meets the eye."

"It'll be that Master Lister," Elizabeth said, sniffing as she wiped her nose with her hand. "I swear he'll be behind all of this."

"But I thought Master Lister was dead. And anyway, I thought he loved Jennet Preston," Jennet pondered aloud. "Alison once told me that he fell in love with her and she had his baby." She cast her mind back over that particular memory. She had been much younger then and had not fully understood the story, but she remembered Alison making a joke about Jennet Preston casting a love spell. Perhaps that's why she's been arrested, Jennet thought. Perhaps someone found out about the love spell.

Old Demdike and Elizabeth looked at the girl, wide-eyed. "Yes child, you're right," Old Demdike said gently. "That particular Master Lister is dead. The Master Lister your mother mentioned is his son, Thomas, now the master of Westby Hall."

"Oh," Jennet replied dumbly. "But why would Master Lister's son want to hurt Jennet?"

"We don't know. Your mother is just guessing," her grandmother replied, giving her a tender smile. "Perhaps because he is upset that his father loved Jennet in the first place. And the way his father died, calling out for Jennet in front of everyone…"

"Mother!" Elizabeth snapped. "I think that's quite enough. Alison had no business telling Jennet anything about poor dear Jennet and Master Lister in the first place. Just wait until I speak to her…"

"I wouldn't be too harsh," Old Demdike replied. "Alison is probably our key to finding out where Jennet Preston is. She hears all sorts of gossip, as well you know."

Elizabeth grimaced. "Aye, that's true enough. I suppose that's what happens when your child goes roaming the country doing God-knows-what with God-knows-who."

Old Demdike glanced briefly at Jennet, as though considering how best to speak in front of the child. "Elizabeth," she began, "you can't keep dwelling on what she gets up to. She's almost grown now; chances are she'll settle down with a husband in the next few years and all will be well."

"With her reputation, I don't think that's likely. Oh Mother, I don't know where I went wrong…" Elizabeth's face began to crumple all over again.

"I know, lass. I know. It's been hard on her, what with her father dying and…everything else that happened back then."

Jennet looked down the table, but she could feel their gazes shift towards her. Everything else that happened back then – she knew that meant her. She happened back then; the source of her mother's shame, the object of Alison's pity, the final nail in John Device's coffin. She sat still, enduring the awkward silence, feeling every last inch of colour drain from her little face. Alison's words to her, spoken with ale-filled fury more than a year ago, rang in her ears: it would have been better if she'd never been born. She winced at the recollection. Did any of them truly love her, she wondered, or were they too busy resenting her for how she reminded them of all the terrible things which had happened to her family?

Jennet was almost glad when the door to Malkin Tower rattled open once again. The wind outside had picked up, casting a cold breeze into their home. Jennet grimaced as a shiver ran through her.

"James, is that you?" Elizabeth called. James had come by some casual labouring work recently and normally returned home in the late afternoon.

"Aye and Alison," he called.

Elizabeth arched an eyebrow. "Well now, I never! Alison Device home at this time. To what do we owe the pleasure, I wonder," she remarked, her voice laden with sarcasm.

"Perhaps that's a good sign," Old Demdike breathed in a hushed tone, patting her daughter on the hand. "Perhaps she's starting to come round. She'll be alright in the end, lass, you'll see."

James walked into the kitchen, followed closely by his sister. "Got any ale?" he asked, licking his dry lips.

Elizabeth shook her head. "Your grandmother had the last drop. You'll have to take a jug down to the stream if you're thirsty."

James screwed up his face in disapproval. "What's for supper?"

"Nothing," their mother replied. "There's nothing left in this kitchen which is fit for the dogs, never mind us. Did you get paid?"

"Not until the end of the week," James replied.

"Well, there will be nothing to eat until then."

Jennet's stomach churned at the thought of the stale bread which lay heavily within it. She pushed her momentary guilt out of her mind. Why should she feel bad, just because she was the only one with any food in her belly, for once?

Alison sat down beside her little sister, jolting Jennet from her thoughts. It wasn't like Alison to join them around the table; she was rarely home at all, and when she was home she usually spent her time in the little room they shared. Jennet studied her sister's face and frowned. She didn't look right; her face was drawn and pale and her eyes were red-rimmed and swollen, as though she had been crying.

Old Demdike also seemed to notice that something was amiss. "Are you alright, Alison? You don't look well. Are you sickening?"

Alison shook her head. "No I'm fine, Grandmother. Just a little tired is all."

"She looked like that when I met her on the lane," James interjected. "Like she'd seen a ghost or something. What's up, sister? Has one of those lads you go about with broken your heart?" he teased, grinning as he lowered his face towards hers.

Without any warning Alison leapt to her feet and gave her brother an almighty shove. The suddenness of her action caught James off guard and he stumbled backwards, crashing into the couple of large pots which sat next to the hearth. "Go to hell, James Device!" she cried. "Burn and rot along with your devil dog!"

Aghast, Jennet stared at Alison as she stomped out of the room, tears streaming down her face. Jennet had rarely ever seen her sister cry, let alone look so upset and angry and…Jennet thought for a moment, trying to find a word for what else she had seen etched upon her sister's face. She didn't know how to describe it – it wasn't a look she'd seen Alison wear before. As young as she was, she knew one thing for certain: Alison was bothered by more than just James's teasing. Something serious had happened to her. Something she wasn't prepared to talk about.

"What on Christ's wounds was all that about?" Old Demdike asked as a dazed-looking James scraped himself off the floor.

Elizabeth Device merely shrugged. "Who knows," she replied. "The stupid girl has probably got herself with child. I suppose it was only a matter of time."

Jennet looked back down at the table, trying to hide the sadness in her eyes. Even after a short lifetime spent at her side, her mother's indifference never ceased to upset her. Sometimes she had to wonder if her mother loved any of them at all.

Jennet spent the rest of the day sitting by the window, watching the evening as it drew in around them, turning to night and shrouding Malkin Tower in the deepest black. Jennet shuddered; as a small child she had feared the dark, exasperating her mother with almost ritual night-time terrors. Although she was older now, if she was honest with herself the night still unnerved her. Jennet tapped her feet anxiously against the stone wall, trying to distract herself from her own fears. The growing darkness brought with it a welcome change in the weather, the earlier wind settling down into a soft breeze. At least she wouldn't be kept awake by a howling gale, Jennet thought. There were still some small mercies she could be thankful for.

That night Jennet slept beside her grandmother, having been

refused entry into the room she and Alison normally shared. Alison had kept up her sullen silence throughout the evening and had not emerged from their room at all, not even to take in the jug of water which James had laid at her door as a sort of peace offering. When it came to bedtime Jennet hadn't complained when her requests to come in so that she could sleep went unanswered. Nor had she complained when her mother had pointed a weary finger in the direction of Grand-mama's room. Some battles, she had come to realise, were not worth fighting.

Her night's sleep was fitful, disturbed by both her grandmother's incessant snoring and the growling of her belly which, having satisfied itself with bread earlier, resumed its usual hungry state. Feeling cross she tossed and turned, her heart pounding hard in her chest as her mind dwelt on her annoyance. She hated trying to sleep on an empty stomach. She hated being poor and never having enough food in the house. She hated that her family's magic seemed to be so effective in so many ways, healing, curing and, she remembered with a shudder, harming others but it was useless at helping them to look after themselves. When she was younger she wanted so much to have magical abilities, to be schooled in her grandmother's cunning ways. Now she wanted nothing to do with it, any of it. What good was that sort of power to her, if she must spend her days living in a crumbling old home, dressed in rags and weakened by hunger?

Eventually Jennet fell into a deep sleep, retreating into one of her favourite dreams; the one where her home was a palace, her dresses fine and trimmed with gold, and her table laden with delicious food. The food was always so vivid that she could smell it, she could taste the rich flavours and savour them as they delighted her senses. After she had eaten she would go outside into her grand gardens, she would walk through the neatly planted rows of giant flowers to the very centre where she would twirl around, dancing and laughing as her dress flared around her. Usually she woke up around then, smiling, her head spinning and her nostrils filled with that sweet floral scent for the briefest of moments, until she remembered where she was and reality took over. The smile, at least, normally lasted a little bit longer.

That morning she was woken by an abrupt banging sound. The noise invaded her dream, blurring the lines between the real and the imagined for a few moments when, to her horror, she saw her fine gardens being trampled by an evil giant made of clay, his heavy stomps destroying her flowers in time with the bang, bang, bang which reverberated in her ears. The confusing vision jolted her from her dream with a start and, with her heart pounding, it took her a few minutes to remember where she was. Beside her, her grandmother continued to snore softly, apparently undisturbed by the noise which seemed to be growing louder and louder.

Curious and frightened, Jennet eased herself out of her blanket and crept to the door, peering through the tiniest crack to see what was going on. Before she could even speculate as to the source of the noise, she saw her mother breeze past and fling the front door of Malkin Tower wide open. She flinched, knowing that her mother would not have appreciated being so rudely awoken.

"Yes?" she heard Elizabeth Device demand.

"Elizabeth Device?" a man's voice asked.

"Yes," she replied, her tone a little meeker now. Clearly she recognised whoever it was standing before her.

"My name is Henry Hargreaves. I am the local constable, and this is Abraham Law of Halifax."

"Yes Master Hargreaves, I know who you are. But why are you here, and why have you brought this stranger to my door?"

Henry Hargreaves cleared his throat. "Goodwife Device, I'm afraid I come on unpleasant business. I have come for your daughter, Alison Device, to arrest her."

"Arrest her?" Elizabeth repeated, stunned. "God's death, what are you talking about? Arrest her for what?"

"There's no need for alarm, Goodwife Device. The sheriff must simply discharge his duty in this matter and ask your daughter some questions. If she can satisfy his enquiries, she will not be away from you for long."

"What questions? What has she been accused of?" Elizabeth demanded to know.

The constable cleared his throat. "She is to be questioned by the sheriff, Master Nowell, at Read Hall. She has been accused of laming this man's father, a pedlar from Halifax by the name of John Law."

"Laming him?" Elizabeth repeated, incredulous. "Alison can have done no such thing. What on earth do you mean, she lamed him?"

There was a brief pause. "I think you know fine well what I mean, Goodwife Device. Your daughter is accused of harming this man through witchcraft."

Those words hit Jennet so hard that it felt as though someone had punched her in the gut. She sank down behind the door, at once horrified, shocked and afraid. Alison, her sister Alison, the one person in the family that Jennet had not suspected of any heinous deeds, was being arrested for witchcraft, a crime for which she could hang. Suddenly, Alison's behaviour over the previous evening made sense – the anger, the tears, the uncharacteristic silence. She had been upset, but she had also been afraid. That look she had on her face when she stormed from the room, the one Jennet didn't recognise at the time, had been fear. She had known that she had done something awful, and she had known that it was only a matter of time before the constable came looking for her.

Jennet put her head in her hands as the first of her tears began to fall. Oh Alison, she thought, what have you done?

8

Spring 1612
'Always Questions'

A solitary tear rolled down Jennet's face as she sat outside the door to Malkin Tower. The day was warm and bright, the sun shining down from a clear blue cloudless sky. In the past Jennet would have rejoiced, knowing that a long day playing outside beckoned her, freeing her from the confines of Malkin Tower's stone walls. Freeing her from her mother's lectures, her sister's jibes and her brother's teasing. Freeing her from her world, just for a little while.

Nowadays, however, Jennet felt anything but free. She frowned, wiping her eyes with the back of her hand as she sought to find the words for how she did feel. So much had happened over the last few weeks, so many terrible things, that her mind was still reeling from it all. Her sister's arrest had been upsetting enough. Jennet shuddered at the memory of Alison being hauled away, her pale face etched with guilt and terror. They had heard little since, the only news coming when the constable returned three days later to arrest her grandmother.

"Alison has confessed to her crime," Henry Hargreaves confirmed. "Just as she did the day before her arrest. She went to visit him, you know – the pedlar, that is. His son took her to visit him while he was convalescing in Colne."

Elizabeth Device had been tight-lipped at the revelation. "I never have known half of what my eldest daughter gets up to," she replied, her tone tinged with bitterness.

"Well apparently she threw herself down at his feet and begged forgiveness, so clearly she knows that she is guilty." The constable paused, drawing a heavy breath. "And now the sheriff has some questions for Goodwife Southerns, too."

"What questions? What is my mother being accused of?" Elizabeth demanded to know.

"Just some questions which have arisen in the course of the sheriff's enquiries. She won't be gone for long," came the constable's only reply, an effortless lie which rolled freely from his tongue. He had said this when he'd come for Alison, too.

The memory of watching her grandmother being taken away made Jennet's lip tremble. More tears fell. Grand-mama hadn't looked frightened like Alison – she had seemed obstinate, almost serene, like she knew that this was coming. Like she had been expecting it all of her life.

The time since her grandmother's arrest had passed in a fog of fear and confusion. The constable had returned once more, on the morning of Maundy Thursday and just days after Old Demdike had been taken away, to inform them that both Alison and her grandmother had been sent to Lancaster gaol to await their trial for witchcraft. Old Chattox and her daughter, Anne, were apparently being held on the same charges, too.

"Well, it's about time," Elizabeth Device had muttered upon learning the fate of their old foes from West Close. But under the circumstances, even she couldn't bring herself to crow about it.

As the news sank in, however, her mother's mood took an unmistakable turn for the worse, swinging uncontrollably between fits of temper and floods of tears. James, meanwhile, had been very quiet, keeping out of his mother's and little sister's way as much as he could manage. When Jennet had seen him, she had noted how tired he looked, his eyes heavy and underlined by dark circles and his posture hunched. She couldn't help but wonder how much of his shrunken appearance was due to his fears for his relatives, and how much of it was because he was weighed down by worry for himself. After all, Jennet reminded herself, he was no less guilty of witchcraft than Grand-mama or Alison. For that matter, he was no less guilty than their mother, either.

Jennet fiddled absentmindedly with a twig, brushing it along the ground so that it made swirling patterns in the dust. She let out a heavy sigh as she wiped her eyes once more. She was beyond knowing what to do with herself. Every day rolled wearily into the next, each one equally tedious and dreadful as they all waited for whatever would happen now.

Each morning Jennet would wake alone in an empty bed, an immediate reminder that her sister was gone and an instant prompt to make her wonder over and over again at what Alison had done. How could Alison have bewitched that man? How did she have such power? Jennet's mind always wandered back to the events of last summer, when Henry Bulcock had accused Alison of bewitching his child. Grand-mama had been adamant that Alison couldn't have done it, even though Alison had all but confessed. If the constable was to be believed, she had confessed this time, too. Was it possible that she was mistaken now, as well as then? Or was she in fact a witch who had never been mistaken at all?

Jennet would climb out of bed then, moping towards the kitchen as her thoughts turned to her grandmother. Old Demdike – the devil woman, someone whose reputation certainly preceded her. Whilst she harboured doubts about Alison's magical abilities, she had no such feelings about her grandmother. Memories of that overheard conversation about Tibb and the miller Baldwin plagued Jennet's mind. Grand-mama had admitted to cursing him and his daughter had died; try as she might, Jennet could not pretend to herself that this had not been her grandmother's doing. She wondered if that was why the sheriff wished to question her, or if she had been accused of something else. Then she realised it might be better if she didn't know.

Her mother could usually be found standing over the hearth, trying to make a pottage from whatever scant vegetables and grain she'd managed to come by. Since the arrests Elizabeth had increasingly confined herself to their kitchen, sometimes doing little more than staring vacantly at an empty pot over a cold hearth. Jennet would always bid her mother good morning, offering up a meek smile in the vain hope that it might do something, anything to lighten the mood. Her efforts were almost always met by silence and a glimpse of the tortured expression which was permanently etched upon her mother's face. Before the morning was even over, Jennet had normally made herself scarce. Solitude, she had realised long ago, was preferable to dealing with other people's foul tempers, their tears and their unkind words. That had never been more true than it was now.

So Jennet sat, day after long day, staring at the wall of her room or gazing at the ground, making circles in the dust while she lost herself to her thoughts and tried to make sense of what she felt. Mostly she was terrified, her chest heavy with the sense of impending doom. After all, she reasoned, the constable had already come for her sister and grandmother, how soon would it be until he came for her mother and brother, too? And if he came for them, what would become of her? Would she be hauled before the sheriff, too? Would she be considered guilty by association? Would she be imprisoned in Lancaster gaol?

However, there was another feeling which plagued her, one which she couldn't quite fathom. Sometimes it was as though her mind was playing tricks upon her, as though it was allowing her to forget the awful things her family had done, making her focus instead on the sheer horror of what faced them now. As young as she was, Jennet was in no doubt as to the severity of her sister's and grandmother's crimes; if they were found guilty, they could hang and if they were hanged, they would be dead. If she was honest with herself, this was the real cause of her tears – the fear that all this would lead them to their deaths. Despite all the terrible things they had done, they were her family and she loved them. She couldn't bear the thought of having to live without them.

Jennet stared out across the rolling fields which flowed down like a river from where Malkin Tower sat. Outside it was still and quiet, with not a soul in sight. No disturbances, no distractions. Jennet sighed. She had always been so good at amusing herself, at inventing games, at finding fun amidst the never-ending drama of the Device household. Right now, however, she found that she couldn't bring herself to do anything. There was no fun to be found, not when things at home were so dire. Not when her family's lives hung in the balance.

The only brief reprieve had come on Good Friday when, much to her surprise, her mother had gone ahead with arranging their annual gathering. Every year they invited their small group of friends to their home on Good Friday to enjoy a modest feast in celebration of the holy day. It was an old tradition, her grandmother had once told her, something which many families had done when she was a little girl.

"I'm sure it's less common now," Old Demdike had said, "what with all these new religious ways. But it's something I like to do."

Jennet had never really understood the remark; the ways of the Church, old and new, were all fairly mysterious to her. However, she liked it when the house was full of laughter, when there was food on the table and ale in their jugs – in the past their gathering had provided those things, and for Jennet it had always been one of the highlights of the year. This year she had expected it not to take place, for it to be forgotten in the upset and trauma of everything that had happened. Her mother and James, however, seemed to have other ideas.

"We need our friends at times like this," her mother had said as she wiped her eyes after yet another fit of tears. "And besides, your grandmother would have wanted us to carry on as normal."

James, apparently enthused by the welcome distraction, had gone out on Maundy Thursday afternoon and stolen a sheep. "Look what I've got for us!" he cried, his tone triumphant, almost euphoric. "What a feast we shall enjoy!"

Jennet had smiled sadly. In the past the sight of that enormous sheep would have delighted her. Now all she could think was that they would be feasting in their home filled with their friends while her sister and grandmother sat shivering in a horrid gaol cell, dreading their fate.

In spite of the difficult circumstances, the gathering began well. Jennet's mother had worried that some of their friends might stay away, fearing association with a family tainted by witchcraft accusations. Happily, however, most of them came and her mother had been so pleased to see them, especially Jennet Preston who had turned up unannounced almost immediately after being released from gaol. Elizabeth had flung her arms around her friend, thanking God over and over again and marvelling that she had come all this way so soon after her ordeal. Jennet had silently rejoiced that kind, smiling Jennet Preston had not been found guilty.

"Of course she isn't guilty," Elizabeth kept saying to anyone who would listen to her. "Just like my mother and daughter aren't guilty. Jennet's trial was all that terrible Master Lister's doing. We must pray that justice is served for my family, just as it was for Jennet."

Jennet Preston's sudden appearance certainly brightened her mother's mood. She drank liberal amounts of ale and danced and sang like she hadn't a care in the world, greeting her guests with kind words and open arms. Jennet caught herself smiling as she remembered how her mother had flung her arms around her half-brother, Christopher, when he arrived with his family. Uncle Christopher hadn't quite known where to put himself. Her mother had even kept a cuddle for her youngest child, and Jennet had relished the rare chance to be enveloped in her mother's arms.

"Ah – my youngest, my little girl. God forbid they take you from me as well," her mother had said, fresh tears welling in her eyes as she stroked her daughter's hair.

The tenderness of the moment had caught Jennet off guard. Recent events had taken their family through many strange twists and turns, but at that moment Jennet thought nothing was quite so unbelievable as the sudden warming of Elizabeth Device's cool heart.

A sudden breeze swept over, swirling the dusty ground on which Jennet sat and blowing grit into her eyes. She let out a pained yelp, rubbing her face as her mind turned to what else had happened that day. Needless to say that given the circumstances of the gathering, everyone had very quickly got very drunk. Jennet recalled how the conversation had become extremely volatile, with inebriated guests consoling themselves with far-fetched plans to acquire some gunpowder and blow a hole in the wall at the Lancaster gaol so that Demdike and Alison could be free once again. Jennet had listened, simultaneously aghast and fascinated by these suggestions. Were they being serious, or was it simply the ale talking?

"Just as long as you leave Old Chattox and Anne Redfearne behind to rot, I don't mind what you try and do!" Elizabeth had seethed. The other guests might have been making a joke, but there was no doubt that her mother was serious about that.

Jennet had retreated to her corner then, made weary by the heady, ale-fuelled atmosphere in the cottage. Jennet Preston had chosen that moment to take her leave as well, heading off back down the hill on her old foal. Her departure had prompted a fresh discussion of Jennet's trial, accompanied by some colourful language about Master Lister and how he had so obviously victimised Jennet for no other crime than being in love with his father.

"You'd think Master Lister would let it drop after all this time," a woman called Katherine Hewit said. She was the wife of a clothier from Colne from whom her mother took in work from time to time. She was also a familiar face, attending almost every Device gathering over the years.

"Hmm," Elizabeth Device mused in response.

"I mean, his father's been dead for five years now," Katherine continued. "It's a terrible business. I've known Jennet for years, you know, ever since I started putting carding and spinning work out to her. The poor woman has suffered enough."

"Aye, she has," Elizabeth lamented. "'I should like to see that Master Lister get what he deserves. He wanted to see Jennet hang – well, it should be him dangling from the end of a rope, not her."

Upon hearing that remark, Jennet had put her fingers in her ears. Over the years of her short lifetime she had seen and heard enough. She no longer had the stomach for that sort of callous talk, even if the wicked gentleman in Gisburn did deserve it.

Jennet's thoughts were interrupted by the faint thud of horses' hooves blown towards her on the gentle breeze. She looked around, rubbing her eyes which were still bothered by the grit. She felt her heart begin to beat faster as she frantically tried to find the source of the noise. Very few people simply passed by their home, tucked away in that remote corner of Blacko hillside. The sound of hooves usually signalled the approach of visitors. It used to be a happy sound, one which Jennet relished, indicating the imminent arrival of a friend or acquaintance bringing work, news, or simply paying a visit. Jennet Preston always arrived on horseback, as did the men who worked for the Hewits when they arrived with some spinning work for her mother. A niggling feeling in Jennet's gut told her that it wasn't either of them, that instead whoever approached Malkin Tower came on much less pleasant business. This was how it was now; visitors were no longer welcomed but dreaded. Jennet looked around once more as the sound drew nearer. Who is coming, she wondered. And what do they want with us now?

Then, riding hard up the hillside, she saw them: two men, better dressed than herself but not fine, not gentlemen. As they drew closer she recognised one of them as the constable Henry Hargreaves, who she'd glimpsed on his last visit on Maundy Thursday. Her heart sank into the depths of her stomach as she spied the serious, determined expression upon his face, the air of being on official business radiating from him as he slowed his horse. The other man was not familiar to her at all; like the constable he wore a stern look, but unlike the constable he looked less sure of himself, his posture a little awkward as though he felt himself to be out of place. Taking his cues from the constable he ordered his horse to trot and side by side they made the final approach to Malkin Tower. Jennet stared at them, frozen to the spot. She couldn't move. She couldn't breathe.

"Good morrow to you - Jennet, isn't it?" the constable said as he dismounted from his horse. He flashed a forced smile in her direction. "Is your mother at home?"

Jennet looked at him, her eyes wide with fear and disbelief. Until now, whenever the constable had called she had been inside Malkin Tower, able to eavesdrop at a safe distance while her mother answered the door. She had never had to encounter him, let alone speak to him directly. Now, faced with his question and the steely, determined way he looked at her as he awaited her answer, she felt overwhelmed. Here was someone with power, someone with authority and she was merely Jennet Device – she was small, she was unimportant, she was vulnerable.

"Jennet," he repeated her name. "We need to speak with your mother. Where is she?"

Both men took a step forward. Instinctively Jennet moved backwards, trying futilely to block the doorway, as if a poor, underfed girl could manage to take up sufficient space to do so. Once again she wished she was bigger, she wished she was stronger. She wished she could send these men away; she wished that she had the power to conjure a storm from the gentle spring breeze and simply get rid of them on a great gust of wind. But she couldn't. She couldn't make them leave, and she couldn't stop what was happening to her family. She was the one being blown along like a helpless speck of dust.

"Mama!" she cried out. "Mama! Please come!"

"God's teeth, child, what is it?" Elizabeth Device called, wiping her hands on her apron as she walked towards the door. Seeing the two men standing there, she stopped dead in her tracks.

Slowly, Jennet turned around, swallowing hard as her eyes came to rest on her mother's face. It was a difficult sight to behold. She looked ghastly; the colour had drained from her already pale skin, and her expression was a pained mixture of horror, dread and acceptance. Her eyes, which were already swollen from frequent bouts of crying, bulged with fear. Folk had often been unkind about her mother's appearance, calling her squinting Lizzy because one of her eyes sat lower on her face and struggled to focus as it should. Grand-mama had once blamed the lifetime of mockery for why her mother could be so prickly.

"When people are cruel to you all the time, being so defensive becomes second nature," she had said. "After a while you can forget how to let your defences down, even with those who care about you. Your mother loves us all; she just has a hard time showing it sometimes."

A lump grew in Jennet's throat as it occurred to her that she would rather have the hard-natured version of her mother than this shrunken, defeated spectacle which now stood before her.

Elizabeth Device drew a deep breath. "Good morrow, constable," she said, greeting the other man with a brief nod.

"They're asking for you, Mama," Jennet muttered meekly, as though any explanation were needed.

"Indeed," she responded, wrapping her arms around herself as though she was suddenly chilled. "Indeed."

The constable took another step forward. "Goodwife Device, I…"

Delicately, Elizabeth raised her hand, stemming the flow of the constable's words. "You have come for the rest of us, then," she said. She spoke quietly and without emotion, her words more of a statement than a question.

The constable nodded. "Yes," he said quietly, his expression grave. "Some matters have arisen in the course of the sheriff's enquiries. There are some questions he wants you to answer."

"Indeed. There are always questions," Elizabeth said, staring impassively at the two men. The constable seemed to recoil, as though her sudden indifference unnerved him.

"Mama, what's happening..." Jennet began. At that moment she didn't know what frightened her more; the presence of these men or the apparent resignation of her mother. Why didn't she fight, why didn't she scream and shout like she always did?

"Yes," replied the constable. "I'm sure you won't be gone for long."

That now familiar assurance seemed to awaken Elizabeth Device from her trance. "A lie. A lie!" she yelled, her eyes growing wild. "We will never come back here! We will never see our home again!" She began to wail and weep, flinging herself around uncontrollably as she railed against these men. "You are liars! Murderers and liars!"

Oddly, her mother's sudden outburst seemed to put the constable at his ease and he immediately sprang into action. "Fetch the boy," he said to the other man as he took Elizabeth firmly by the arm and began to escort her away. "And bring the little girl too. It's time to go."

"Go where?" Jennet cried. "Go where? And why?"

But no one answered her. No one would tell her where they were going. No one would tell her what questions they were expected to answer or what the sheriff had discovered. It was just as it had been for all of her life: no one would tell her anything at all.

James emerged from their home moments later, his expression fixed somewhere between stunned and terrified. Together they were taken down the hill and loaded into the large, rickety-looking cart which awaited them on the lane. Her mother had fallen silent by then, her violent sobs reduced to little more than soft sniffles. Jennet glanced at her mother's pitiful face, her brother's vacant stare. Her stomach churned. They had both given in, she realised; they were both too weary or too guilty to fight anymore. They knew, as she knew, that beyond the sheriff's questions lay accusations, arrest and imprisonment – that was what had happened to Alison, then to Grand-mama, and now it was happening to them. One way or another, this was the end of it all;

the end of clay pictures, of talking animals, of muttered curses. The end of love spells, of cures for sick cows or remedies for ailing people. The end of the power and magic which had surrounded Jennet, which had been there all of her life.

Jennet clasped her hands together as the cart set off, the first of her warm tears trickling down her face as she looked back at Malkin Tower, the only home she had ever known. That simple, crumbling stone cottage had borne witness to it all; the feasts and gatherings, the boredom of rainy days, the heat of family arguments, the idle gossip, the laughter and the tears. It would never again contain their stories and their secrets - those things were to be flung out into the world now, to be questioned and examined, to be criticised and condemned.

Yes, Jennet thought, this was the end of everything, the end of life as she had always known it. The question was, what would become of her now?

9

Summer 1612
'A Fine Petticoat'

The dress was so beautiful that Jennet could not take her eyes off it. It was the most glorious thing she'd ever seen, the petticoat fashioned in a deep red and paired with a contrasting green bodice. She had never seen clothing coloured so brightly, let alone worn it. She was a girl used to hand-me-downs from her elder sister, bland items of beige and grey, frayed with age and ragged at the edges. She was not used to clothing like this. She loved the petticoat the most, and had gasped with delight when Mistress Nowell had brought it to her the previous night.

"A gift from the master," she'd said with a small smile.

"Oh thank you!" she'd cried. "It's so bright! Just like my leaves!"

The mistress had frowned a little, not understanding the remark but not asking for clarification either. She'd left Jennet again then with a brief nod and a swift click of her bedroom door. Jennet hadn't minded; she'd nothing much to say to Mistress Nowell. She was a quiet lady, pleasant enough but fairly aloof, with nice manners but not a great deal of conversation. She seemed to accept the presence of this young girl in her home without complaint, but showed about as much interest in her as she would show in one of her servants. In short, she was nothing like Master Nowell. Master Nowell would want to hear all about how much she loved the dress and how it reminded her of the bright leaves she used to collect along the lane.

The sun shone down upon the courtyard as Jennet twirled round and round, admiring the dress as it swished and shimmered in the light. The summer had been long and hot, and Jennet had spent as many of her days as possible outside. The courtyard was her favourite place to be, with its bright paths and well-organised shrubbery providing plenty of space for running, for dancing, for whatever she felt like doing. It suited Master Nowell for her to play out there, too.

"You must stay close to the house," he'd said. "So the courtyard is perfect. We can't have you wandering off."

The master was rarely at home during the day, and so Jennet was often left to her own devices. She was used to this, of course; it was the way her life had always been, although of course until she came to stay at Read Hall she had kept herself occupied in far less sumptuous surroundings. That was one thing of which she would never tire, the richness and finery of Read Hall providing her with endless amusement and wonder. She had never been able to imagine that people really lived in homes such as this. To her, Read Hall was the stuff of stories and she was like a princess living in the castle. It was the fuel for her imagination; the setting for endless magical tales and wondrous games of which she could never grow bored.

Nonetheless, as time wore on she would often wish the hours away, hoping that the time would soon come when Master Nowell would return home, signalling the beginning of their evening routine. He usually arrived back in time for supper which he would take in the dining room with the mistress before retiring to his library. After spending a little time dealing with his papers and attending to his various important affairs, he would summon Jennet to join him and she would be escorted down the grand hallway by a maid, trying to resist the urge to skip. Upon arriving in the library he would invite her to sit down and she'd choose her favourite seat, the deepest one adorned with the most beautiful embroidery. She'd wait quietly then; she'd learned early on that Master Nowell would choose the course of the conversation, but that she would get her opportunity to speak and, most importantly of all, the indulgence of being listened to.

"Mistress Nowell tells me you have spent the day outside," he'd often begin, his remark an invitation for her to tell him all about her day's adventures. He'd smile, listening attentively as she reeled off details of her games, imaginings and discoveries with enthusiasm.

"It is such a pleasure to see you enjoying your time with us so much, Jennet," he'd say, rubbing his grey beard in that way he always did when he was thinking. Jennet would nod in agreement, giving him her broadest smile. One day, she told herself, she would find the words to tell him how much she loved Read Hall. One day she would pluck up the courage to tell him how much she wanted to stay.

Master Nowell would usually change the subject then, steering her young mind towards whatever was occupying his thoughts that evening. Often he would want to ask her questions; questions about her family, questions about what she had seen and heard at home. When she had first been brought to Read Hall she had been very reluctant to answer these questions. Jennet shuddered as she remembered how she'd cowered, her whole body shaking with fear as she stood in front of this towering, esteemed gentleman in his fine home. For those first few days she'd refused to speak. She had been too frightened – of this man, of this house, of being completely alone after being separated from her mother and brother. More than anything, she realised, she'd been frightened to tell him anything, in case she made things worse for her family. After all, as Grand-mama had told her once, saying things could be dangerous.

Master Nowell had been endlessly patient with her, filling her silences with easy conversation about himself, about his family and his home. He would show her interesting things – books he owned, trinkets he had collected, and he would tell her stories about them. He would tell her other things, too, things she'd never really thought about before. He talked to her about being the sheriff, about the importance of the law, about the importance of truth, and God and the Church. He talked to her of the importance of things which had never been very important to her at all. Slowly but surely his words had drawn her out of herself, her guard lowering, her fear diminishing as she engaged instead with all these interesting and bewildering ideas and concepts that rolled off his learned tongue.

"Does your mother ever take you to church, Jennet?" he asked her once, just days after she'd arrived.

Jennet had shaken her head. She couldn't see the harm in telling him this, although the mere admission made her feel inexplicably ashamed. "No, Master Nowell. My mother cares little for church. My brother often goes - Grand-mama says he's devout."

"Does your grandmother go with him?"

"No, Master Nowell. She says she's too aged and that she prefers the old ways."

Master Nowell had frowned deeply at this, rubbing his beard for some moments. "It is a great pity that you have not been raised to know the teachings of the Church, Jennet. Those teachings are the code by which we all must live; they are important for the sustenance of our souls, and they are important to law and order, too. You see, if man lives in the Christian way he knows that he should not commit crime. If he is a good Christian, he does not steal, he does not kill, and," he looked at her pointedly, "he does not curse or bewitch his neighbours. If he does stray from the path of righteousness, then he knows that he has done wrong, he knows the danger that his soul is in. For most men, this knowledge is enough to ensure that they obey the law. Do you understand?"

Jennet had nodded slowly. "Yes, Master Nowell." In truth she wasn't sure that she understood at all but she was too embarrassed to admit it.

"My fear for you, Jennet, is that you do not know what is right and what is wrong because you have not received Christ's teachings."

Her face had grown hot at this accusation. "But I do, Master Nowell!" she had protested. "I know what is good and what is bad. I have never done anything wrong," she straightened her posture, feeling indignant. This was the truth: it was the truth and she knew it.

"I am sure you haven't done anything wrong," he'd replied with a smile. "But you have seen others do wrong, haven't you? You have seen and heard some terrible things I am sure."

She had shrunken back down then, her fear returning. Fear of the memories, and fear of the consequences if she talked about them.

"When grave wrongs are done unto others, Jennet, it is the truth that is important," he'd continued. "As it is written in the Book of John, the truth will set you free. Do you wish to be free, Jennet?"

She'd shaken her head. "I'm not sure, Master Nowell. I don't really know what it means."

He'd given her that gentle smile then, the one which made his face all crinkled and illuminated. If she'd ever known her father or her grandfather, she imagined that was how they would have smiled. "A happy, comfortable life, Jennet, with good people to love and care for you. A life lived in God. A life which does not endanger your soul by exposing you to heresy." The way he'd spat that final word had made her wince. "Is that the sort of life you want?"

She'd smiled too, then, her fear receding at the prospect of such a future. "Yes, Master Nowell."

"In that case, Jennet," he'd replied, "I will need you to answer my questions truthfully, and do as I ask. I know it will be hard but we have many weeks ahead of us to prepare, so take your time. Please don't worry; you are safe here, we will look after you. While you are at Read Hall you shall want for nothing."

Jennet performed a final spin in her dress and sank to the ground as those words rang in her ears. It was certainly true; the Nowells had cared for her well during these past weeks, perhaps better than anyone had ever cared for her. Her filthy, worn clothes had been replaced with newer, warmer items. Her infrequent meals of watery pottage and stale bread had been replaced by regular, wholesome dining. The Nowells ate as though every day was a feast, consuming generous quantities of beef, pork and fish accompanied by delicately prepared vegetables, washed down with ale or wine and followed by cakes and sweetmeats. Jennet delighted in all of the new, unfamiliar tastes she had experienced but above all, she relished the fact that she no longer had to endure the gnawing ache of hunger.

Every evening she went to sleep in a large comfortable bed, well covered with blankets. Sleep usually came easily, aided no doubt by fresh air and a full belly, but it was not always peaceful. Sometimes she would wake in the night, whimpering, her body curled up painfully in a corner of the bed. Her heart would be pounding, her mind bursting with the faces of her family fading away in gaol while she stayed here and betrayed their secrets. She knew that was where they were; Master Nowell had not tried to hide the truth from her.

"Justice must be done, Jennet," he'd said when she'd cried for them. "The evidence against them must be considered by the assizes and until that time, they must remain in Lancaster gaol. It is the proper way of things. The right place for you is here, with me, helping me with my enquiries."

She knew that Master Nowell must be right, of course, but that didn't make her dreams any easier to overcome. She would lie there, wide awake, replaying the last time she saw her mother over and over in her mind, seeing the shock and horror etched across her tired face as her youngest child was torn from her. It was during those moments, the ones which contained her sadness, her guilt and regret, that she felt most alone. She would stretch out in that big bed then, pressing her limbs towards the edges in the hope that she might feel her sister lying there. It was a futile wish, of course. There was no one there - only little Jennet, locked up in luxury and awaiting the day that she must do as Master Nowell wished. She knew there was no avoiding it; she had to speak the truth, she had to save the soul which she was now conscious she had. She had to find a better life. She had to be free.

The problem was, she'd think as she drifted back to sleep, that she didn't really want to be free. She didn't want a better life; she wanted the one she had right here with Master Nowell. Perhaps if she continued to tell him everything, if she answered all of his questions and did everything he asked, he'd let her stay. Perhaps he would be the father she'd never had.

A day spent in the courtyard was followed by a hearty meal of boiled fish and vegetables, which Jennet devoured eagerly. Master Nowell had not returned at his usual time and so after dinner Jennet was taken straight up to her room. She didn't mind; she was feeling so weary after enjoying all that sunshine that she could barely keep her eyes open. As much as she enjoyed Master Nowell's company, she had to admit that a reprieve from answering his questions was a blessed relief. She lay down on her bed with a weary sigh. Normally the prospect of a quiet evening by herself would have been daunting; she hated being confined to her room with nothing to distract her. Tonight, however, nothing was exactly what she wanted to do. She didn't want to think, she didn't want to feel, and she certainly didn't want to talk.

Jennet fell almost immediately into a deep, dreamless slumber, her body and her mind succumbing to their need for complete rest. She didn't hear the maid come in and check on her, clicking her tongue disapprovingly at the fully-clothed young girl strewn across the bed, the day's sweat and dirt still apparent on her face. Nor did she hear the master come home and ask to see her immediately; she didn't hear his hushed voice outside her room, complaining that she was asleep already and insisting that she was awoken at once. She didn't hear anything, in fact, until she was roughly shaken from sleep by the mistress and even then it sounded as though she was hearing her words through water. Everything seemed so far away, so distant – her family, their crimes, Master Nowell's questions – all of it so muffled by sleep that it might as well be at the other side of the world. Jennet couldn't help but wish it could stay that way.

"Master Nowell wishes to see you in his library."

"But I'm so tired…"

"The master insists, Jennet. He has something he needs to tell you."

Those words were enough to jolt Jennet back from the brink of sleep. She followed the mistress down the grand staircase and towards the library, her heart pounding hard and fast in her chest. What did the master wish to speak to her about? What was so important that he felt the need to wake her? Her gut told her that it couldn't be good news – as much as she hoped it might be. There was no such thing as good news anymore, not really. Outside of Read Hall and its impenetrable walls of wealth and riches was her family, festering in gaol as they awaited their trial. All the nice meals and fine dresses in the world couldn't change that, she thought guiltily, no matter how much she enjoyed them.

Jennet rubbed the final vestiges of sleep from her eyes as Mistress Nowell opened the door to the library. She beckoned her inside with a curt wave of her hand.

"She's here, as you requested," she said to her husband. Jennet thought that she sounded a little irritated, but then she supposed she had better things to do in the evening than Master Nowell's bidding. She flinched as she realised that the mistress's tone reminded her of her mother.

"Thank you," replied Master Nowell smoothly, apparently immune to his wife's cross manner.

He sat in his usual position in a grand armchair situated next to the fireplace, with his back facing the door. Normally he would rise when Jennet came into the room, greeting her with a smile.

Tonight he did not get up, not even when the mistress left without another word, closing the door rather too forcefully behind her. An awkward silence descended in the room. Jennet hovered near the door, wondering what she should do.

After a few moments Master Nowell breathed a heavy sigh. "Come here, Jennet," he called. "Come and sit down."

Jennet did as she was told, sitting down obediently in her favourite chair. She looked at him, just as she always did, waiting for him to speak first. She noticed that he looked tired, his lined face drawn and pale, his eyes dark and heavy. He rubbed his face wearily for a moment before taking a long sip from the wine glass sitting beside him, as though its contents might fortify him for what he was about to say. Jennet gulped hard, shifting uncomfortably in her seat as she prepared herself for whatever it was that he had summoned her for.

"I am sorry that I woke you, Jennet," he began. "I'm afraid it has been a rather long day and I am home much later than I expected. I have been attending to some urgent family matters." He paused, drawing his fingers across his eyes once again. "Some difficult matters concerning my son. Your children are always your children," he added with a slow shake of his head. Jennet thought he looked sad – she had never seen him look that way before.

"Anyway," he continued, "none of that needs to concern you. I asked to see you about a different matter. Unfortunately, today I learned some rather regrettable news which I wanted to share with you as soon as I could." He took another sip of wine.

"What is it, Master Nowell?" Jennet asked. Normally she wouldn't dream of prompting him, but tonight she could not bear the sense of dread which was sweeping through her any longer. "Is it my mother?"

"It's your grandmother," he replied. "I'm afraid she's dead, Jennet."

For a moment Jennet just stared at him, blankly, as though she could not comprehend what he was saying, as though it wasn't real. She knew she would see Grand-mama again; she would see her at the trial, just as she would see all of them. Master Nowell had told her so, time and time again, when they discussed the questions he'd ask and recited how she'd answer.

"You will have to face your family again," he'd said. "You're going to have to be brave. Can you be brave?"

Yes, she had agreed. She could be brave. And yet now he was telling her that she'd face one person less, that Grand-mama, the matriarch of their family, wouldn't be there. How could it be so? How could Grand-mama be dead? How was it possible that she'd never see her again? Slowly, a first tear slipped out from under her eye, then another, then another, until they ran like a river down her cheeks. "Grand-mama," she croaked softly.

"Here, child," Master Nowell said, handing her a handkerchief. "Dry your eyes. She was old; old and frail. The elderly often do not fare well in gaol. At least she will not have to stand trial now. You could regard that as a blessing, I suppose."

Jennet shook her head, taken aback by his cold tone. "But she was my grandmother, she was always so good to me, she helped so many folk over the years…"

"And cursed quite a number of them, too," Nowell snapped. He paused for a moment, resting his hands on the arms of his chair as though trying to compose himself. "Jennet," he began again, softening his tone, "we have talked about this at great length – the power to heal is the same as the power to harm. It is unnatural work and such power can only come from the Devil himself. Dear child, you have been exposed to so much sin and heresy that you cannot make sense of it! When I think about those charms you told me…" he shook his head, allowing his voice to trail off.

"Crucifix us hoc signum vitam Eternam, Amen," Jennet replied. "My mother used to say it over the ale when she was brewing. It always gave us good drink," she added.

"Popery," he muttered. "Popery and witchcraft."

"Master Nowell, how is my mother? And my brother and sister, too? How do they fare?" She couldn't stop herself from asking. She had to know.

"I have no news of them," he replied shortly. "Listen, Jennet, I know this has been a shock for you. You have been a very good girl over these past few weeks – you have been very honest and brave. It must be hard for you, to see your family for what they are. I know how terrible it is when your family disappoints you," he added, his expression darkening momentarily as his eyes sank down into his lap.

Jennet gave a grim smile. "It is odd how much I love them, even though they have done so many bad things, even though at times they were cross or unkind…"

Nowell looked up. "Were they unkind to you, Jennet?"

"Sometimes. My mother had a bad temper, and James and Alison liked to taunt me." She bit her lip, realising that she was talking about them as though they were gone forever. "It did upset me, mainly because I always felt different from them. Because I'm not a Device, not really."

"No, that's right," Master Nowell mused. "I recall that being mentioned in your mother's deposition. John Robinson found himself bewitched for daring to speak of it. Your father still lives, doesn't he? A Richard Sellers of White Moor. Do you know your father?"

"No, Master Nowell," Jennet looked down, the familiar feeling of shame returning.

"I see," he replied. "Well, perhaps that is another wrong which can be righted. A better life, Jennet. A happier life, that's what you need, isn't it?"

Jennet beamed. "Yes, Master Nowell."

Master Nowell gulped down the last of his wine. "It's getting late. I think you'd better go to bed."

Jennet nodded as she got up from her chair. "Goodnight, Master Nowell," she said, walking towards the door. A small smile grew on her lips as she remembered what she wanted to say to him earlier, before fatigue and the news of Grand-mama's death overtook her. She turned around, gesturing at her skirts. "Master Nowell, thank you for the new clothes. The petticoat is beautiful."

"You're very welcome," he replied, returning her smile. "Although you can't wear them at the assizes. You will need to look as you always have done. You will have to leave them here."

"Alright," she replied. "But I will be able to come back and get them, won't I? Because they are a gift."

Master Nowell paused for a moment, a curious look passing over his face. "Of course," he said. "I am sure that after the assizes arrangements will be made."

Jennet closed the library door and walked down the hallway. Her heart was once again conflicted with so many swirling, competing emotions. She felt sad, worried, tired, and yet cheered and hopeful all at once. Grand-mama was dead, her family's trial was still looming and she would still have to speak in court against them. All of it made her feel so sorry and sick and yet…Master Nowell had said it himself, arrangements would be made for her. Arrangements which, she felt certain, involved her remaining at Read Hall. Why else would he have said that she could return to get her clothes? After all the hardship, all the traumatic things she had seen and heard, and all the horrid things she must still do, she was sure that life would begin anew. She would do the right thing, she would tell the truth and then she would have a better life. Master Nowell had said so, and she could trust him, she knew she could. After all, Master Nowell cared about her; he wanted her to be happy, he wanted her to be free.

As Jennet climbed back into bed that night she knew that she was no longer on borrowed time. She knew for the first time in her life that she had something to look forward to: her future, right here. Arrangements would be made. Read Hall was her future. Read Hall was her better life.

10

**Summer 1612
'Painting Pictures'**

The courtroom was hot, musty and uncomfortable. Jennet was lifted up on to a table and ordered to stand there so that the court could see her. It was necessary because she was so small, Master Nowell tried to reassure her; hers was the most important story of all and it had to be told, it had to be heard. Nonetheless, standing up there, Jennet felt dizzy and exposed. All she could see before her was a sea of faces, a crowd of inquisitive eyes all fixed upon her, watching, waiting expectantly for what she would say, what insight she would give them into the notorious, sordid world in which she'd lived.

"Look at the little wench," she heard someone say. "There's nothing to her, poor lass."

"What a life she must have had," said another. "What horrors she must have seen."

Horrors. Jennet looked down at her hands, which she clasped together tightly, her palms sweating profusely in the summer heat. What horrors had she seen? In truth she had seen very little, although she had heard a great deal. Her young mind had been filled with stories and confessions; tales of bewitched ale, of talking animals, of clay pictures crumbled into the fire. But she had never actually seen any of these things for herself; she had always been at home, or in her stone hut, or on the lane, or down by the river. She had always been left alone. It was no way to treat a child, Master Nowell had said; to leave her to her own devices while they occupied themselves with their dark practices. It was yet more evidence, he'd said, of her family's predilection for evil.

"All rise in court!" the judge barked, startling Jennet back to her senses.

Jennet watched with wide eyes as her family were led into the courtroom. They were almost beyond recognition; filthy and frail, their hair matted with dirt and their eyes bulging with hunger and fear. Despite her prominent position in the courtroom, none of them looked at her; they seemed dazed, as though they were not really aware of what was going on around them. Or, Jennet thought, they were simply ignoring her as they'd always done.

Behind them walked the other prisoners, a large group of them, some known to her, others not. She narrowed her eyes as she saw Chattox hobble in, leaning heavily on her daughter, Anne. So, the evil Chattox still lived; she had survived Lancaster gaol. Jennet felt angry then, wishing that it had been Chattox who'd perished in there instead of Grand-mama. She had to wonder what was wrong with her; she should have been feeling sorry for the pitiful sight of her mother, her brother, her sister as they stood helplessly awaiting trial. Yet all she could think about was how much she wished that she could see Grand-mama just one more time.

"Proceed with your case, Master Nowell," the judge instructed.

"Yes, my Lord Altham," Master Nowell answered with a brief, courteous bow. "Before you today, my Lord, are nineteen persons, all accused of the most heinous crime of witchcraft. Indeed, the evidence which will be presented before the court today should horrify us all, for it seems that Pendle has been overrun by witches and their devilish practices. You will hear evidence of spells and pictures used to curse, to inflict illness and even death upon unfortunate neighbours. You will hear evidence of spirits and familiars appearing as animals to do the witch's bidding. You will even hear evidence of a witches' Sabbath during which this malevolent assembly plotted yet more death and destruction." Master Nowell paused as the courtroom reacted with murmurs and gasps to what he'd just said.

"Have you the name of the first prisoner you wish to call to the bar?" the judge asked, sounding impatient.

"I do indeed, my Lord," Master Nowell replied. "I call Elizabeth Device, wife of the late John Device of the Forest of Pendle."

A guard nudged Elizabeth forward and tentatively she walked towards the front of the room. Jennet's stomach lurched; her mother looked so pale and unwell. Elizabeth looked up, seeming to notice her child for the first time. There was no smile, not even a hint of relief in her eyes at seeing her youngest child after all these months; there was merely an acknowledgement, frowning and indifferent. Jennet let out a sigh; after all, what else did she expect, given the circumstances?

The judge gestured towards Jennet. "And this young maid is this your witness?" he asked.

"Yes, my Lord. The court shall hear testimony from Jennet Device, daughter of the accused." More gasps around the courtroom.

The frown on Elizabeth Device's face hardened. "No," she insisted, her eyes flitting from Jennet to Master Nowell, the judge and back again. Jennet could only watch as the realisation of what was happening swept over her mother's expression, darkening her features with a look of anger and terror. "No," she repeated, her voice growing louder and more indignant. "Jennet. Jennet! What do you think you're doing? Have you lost your silly little mind? You will get us all killed; you will send us to the gallows, is that what you want? What will become of you then, with no one to look after you? You'll die! You'll rot, you stupid, stupid child!"

The force of her mother's wrath was more than Jennet could bear. She climbed down off the table and turned to Master Nowell, her face crumpling. "I can't do it, Master Nowell. I can't bear to speak against them. Even if it's the truth, I can't bear to say it."

Master Nowell leaned down, his face set with that familiar warm smile. "You must, Jennet. You must. Truth and justice demand that you must tell your story."

Jennet felt herself shrink further. "It's too much…" she began, her voice faltering as the first tears fell. "It's too hard to say it…to talk about it in front of my mother. It was different telling you, Master Nowell. It was different when I was at Read Hall, away from my family…"

Master Nowell gave a brief nod. "I understand, Jennet. I can ask for your mother to be removed from the courtroom so that you can give your evidence. Would you like me to do that?"

Jennet sniffed. "Yes. I think that would help."

"Alright," he replied, giving her a reassuring pat on the back. "I will speak to the judge. Don't worry, Jennet. Whatever happens, all will be well. Your mother is wrong; there are those who care for you, who will look after you once this is all over. Arrangements will be made, remember?"

"Yes, I remember." Jennet gave him a weak smile. She knew she had to keep his promise in her mind. It would help her to get through the difficult hours ahead.

A brief word with the judge was all it took to see her mother swiftly removed. She did not go quietly of course. "Damn you, child! Damn you to hell!" were her parting words. Jennet tried her best not to shudder as she was lifted back up on to the table.

"So, Jennet, I think we may now proceed," Master Nowell continued, his voice seamless and completely unshaken by the events of the past few minutes. "Please tell the court when you first discovered that your mother was a witch."

Jennet took a deep breath, readying herself to recite the lines she had practised so often in Read Hall's fine library. "My mother is a witch," she began, "and I know this to be true. Three years ago she summoned Ball, her spirit who takes the likeness of a brown dog, to help her kill John and James Robinson of Barley…"

Once the first words were out, it all became a little easier. Jennet focussed on the task at hand, reeling off stories overheard, tales told and names ill-wished as she identified her family's victims. One by one, each of her family members were called to take the stand and, when prompted by Master Nowell, she duly gave her evidence against them. When it came to James's turn she spoke at length about the bewitchment and death of Mistress Towneley. During her time at Read Hall, Master Nowell had been very interested in this particular story, going over it with her repeatedly. It was important, he'd said; after all, Jennet had seen for herself how upset James was at his treatment by the mistress of Carr Hall. She had also borne witness to his admission that the Devil had spoken to him through his dog, instructing him as to how to exact his revenge.

"That your brother crumbled a clay image of this woman over the fire in order to bring about her demise is the gravest example of devilish practices," he had mused. "Did you see her again, before she died? Did you see how ill she looked?"

Jennet shook her head. "No, Master Nowell. I had no cause to go to Carr Hall after the day that the mistress struck James for stealing her turves."

"Well," he'd replied with a slow rub of his hands. "It would be better if you had seen her. As a witness, Jennet, you need to build a picture of what took place. Perhaps you saw her in her kitchen, a week or so before her death, looking unwell. Perhaps that's what you saw."

The only time James's stony face flinched in court was when she repeated this part of her story. His eyes, which until then had stared straight ahead, shifted briefly towards her in a look which told her that he knew that part was a lie. A pang of guilt surged through Jennet's gut then, but only briefly. After all, she reassured herself, the rest of it was true: he had bewitched and murdered Mistress Towneley. She was merely painting a better picture of the truth; Master Nowell had told her so himself.

If painting pictures was really important, then there was no better picture than the one she created of the gathering at Malkin Tower on Good Friday. Master Nowell had prepared her to answer extensive questions on her family's feast, coaching her in the exact descriptions she should use, the information and proceedings that she must make sure to include. Jennet felt most at ease talking about this; unlike many of the deeds she had to testify to, she had seen this for herself and knew exactly what had happened. At Read Hall Master Nowell had, of course, educated her on its true nature: it was not a mere feast, he had told her, but a witches' Sabbath.

"All those who attended were friends of your family, each guilty of their own dark practices," he had said. "Therefore, it is very important that you can tell the court exactly who was there, and confirm what the purpose of the gathering was."

In court, just as they had rehearsed in his library, he drew this information from her. She talked and talked, telling the court about how her brother had stolen a sheep and how they had dined on beef, bacon and roasted mutton. She told them how around twenty of her family's friends and acquaintances had attended, reeling off a great long list of them, taking great care not to leave anyone out. As she gave her lengthy descriptions she began to relax; she could feel the court warming to her, impressed by her recollections, hanging on every word she said. For a moment she almost forgot why she was there; she forgot that her family were on trial for their lives and that her words were damning them, edging them ever closer to the gallows. Instead she allowed herself to bask in the limelight. She had never had so many people actually listening to her before, why should she not enjoy it? After all, everything she had to say was true and as Master Nowell had told her so many times, it was the truth that was important.

The only time Jennet almost stumbled was when the judge decided to cross-examine her, forcing her to depart from her well-remembered script.

"Can you repeat the names of the women who were there?" he asked her. "Can you pick each of them out from the line of the accused?"

Jennet nodded. "Of course, my Lord Altham," she replied, recovering herself. She was lifted down from the table and walked along the line, naming each of them in turn.

"And are you certain that Alice Nutter was in attendance?" the judge asked her.

Jennet nodded again. "Yes, my Lord Altham." She approached Alice Nutter and took the fine, proud woman by the hand. She had always been one of her mother's more unusual acquaintances, a woman of far better manners and means than the lowly Devices. Her hands were cold, but not as icy as her stare which bore down on Jennet, unrelenting in its despair and resignation. Jennet merely shrugged at her. Well you were there, Mistress Nutter, she thought. You were there and that is the truth.

"And do you know Joan of Style?" the judge asked her. "Was she there? Can you point her out to me?"

One glance at Master Nowell told Jennet what her answer must be. The truth; only the truth would do. "No, my Lord," she replied seamlessly. "No such woman was there. I have never heard that name."

"Very good," said the judge with a smile, apparently satisfied that his examination and little trap had proven Jennet's testimony to be reliable. "You may continue with your witness, Master Nowell."

"Thank you, my Lord," Master Nowell replied, before turning back to address Jennet, who had been restored to her table-top pedestal. "Your brother James testified in his deposition that the purpose of this gathering was to name your sister Alison's familiar and to plot to free Elizabeth Southerns alias Old Demdike, Alison Device, Anne Whittle alias Chattox and her daughter Anne Redfearne from Lancaster gaol by blowing up the castle. And of course, to help Jennet Preston of Gisburn exact her revenge on Master Thomas Lister of Westby Hall." Master Nowell's eyes shifted briefly towards the judge. "For the court's information, this latter matter has been considered by York assizes. Would you agree with your brother's deposition, Jennet?"

"Yes," Jennet replied, nodding passively, a small frown passing briefly over her face. She wondered what Master Nowell had meant about the York assizes; this was the first time she had heard about this. Of course, she was in no position to ask. She knotted her fingers anxiously for a moment. Jennet Preston had always been so kind to her. She hoped that she wasn't in any trouble.

Jennet recalled the first time Master Nowell presented her with her brother's testimony during her time at Read Hall. It had seemed very specific, painting the gathering as some sort of controlled meeting rather than the bit of merriment and solace it was meant to be. But then, she did recognise some of the things he talked about; she remembered closing her ears to the wild talk of gunpowder and her mother's wish to see Master Lister hang. Who knew what else was talked about afterwards? If James had told him that these matters were what they ultimately discussed, it must be true, even if the impression it gave seemed a little incomplete. Now, standing there in court, she felt overcome with the urge to elaborate, to tell the court that their gathering had always been such a happy event and that in many ways, and despite everything that had happened, this year had been no different.

"We did have a feast every Good Friday, though," she began. "It was my grandmother's wish…"

"Thank you, Jennet," Master Nowell said, his tone a little curt. Jennet flinched. She had spoken out of turn, departing from what they had agreed she should say, and in doing so she had upset Master Nowell. Her mother was right; she was a silly girl.

"Have you finished with your witness, Master Nowell?" the judge asked.

"Yes, my Lord Altham. The witness may retire."

Jennet was lifted down from the table and led away. She glanced behind her, drawing a sharp breath as she took in the pale, frightened faces of her family one more time. I had no choice, she thought, hoping beyond hope that they could somehow read her mind. The truth had to be told. Her eyes wandered back to Master Nowell. He had his back turned to her as he gathered his papers in readiness for questioning the next prisoner. He did not turn around; he did not look at her or smile or nod. He was angry, of course he was. He had no further business with her now. She walked away, led by the guards, sadness engulfing her. She was sad for her family, of course, and sad about what she had just had to do. But more than anything, she realised, no longer having Master Nowell's attention made her saddest of all.

A full day passed before Jennet was recalled to court once more. She hadn't been allowed to hear the rest of the trials, and once her evidence had been heard she had been kept locked in a small room in the castle, not uncomfortable but painfully bare, providing little distraction. The room also had no windows, meaning Jennet couldn't tell whether it was day or night. She slept fitfully, waking only to take the meals which were shoved inside three times a day. The food was thin and poor quality, a far cry from what she had grown accustomed to at Read Hall.

"At least they're feeding you," a guard remarked once as he pushed a bowl of watery pottage towards her.

Jennet wanted to remind him that of course they should; she wasn't a prisoner, after all. But she didn't have the energy. Every last ounce of her will and spirit had been used up during the trial. She had nothing left to give. And so, after eating, she slept.

On the morning that the guard returned, telling her that she was to come with him, she felt a little confused. She squinted at him in the bright daylight which had flooded in through the wide open door. "Do I need to speak in court again?" she asked, searching her mind for some unspoken phrase, some untold story which she had omitted. "I thought I told them everything."

"Oh, you did," the guard replied with a small chuckle. "It's time for the verdicts – you know, it's time for the judge to tell the prisoners their fate. Better hurry up – the court will be busy. Always is when it comes to the sentencing."

She was led into the courtroom and told to sit down on a bench. Her position was a far-cry from the table-top prominence of her witness stand, but Jennet felt glad of it. She no longer craved the attention; she no longer wanted anyone to notice her. She just wanted to shrink into a corner and find out her family's fate. Whatever was going to happen, she just wanted this all to be over.

Jennet watched in a daze as, one by one, the prisoners were recalled to the bar. She held her breath as her mother took the stand, her body so frail that she could barely hold it upright, let alone walk. The judge gave her a withering look as she hobbled over, before turning his attention to the jury.

"Good gentleman of the jury, have you reached a verdict?" he asked.

A juryman rose to his feet. "We have, my Lord," he replied with a brief bow.

"And do you find Elizabeth Device, wife of the late John Device of the Forest of Pendle, guilty or not guilty of the murders by witchcraft of John Robinson and James Robinson, and colluding with her mother Elizabeth Southerns, now deceased, and Alice Nutter in the murder of Henry Mitton, as contained in the indictment against her?"

"We find Elizabeth Device guilty on all counts," the jurymen replied.

Jennet could only watch as the judge spared no redundant words on her mother; his judgement was passed as swiftly as it was harsh.

"Elizabeth Device," he barked. "In accordance with the law of this land, you are sentenced to be hanged by the neck until you are dead."

These were the words that Jennet heard over and over again, first to her mother, then her brother, then her sister. She could only watch with a heavy heart as Alison wept, begging the judge and the jury to spare her life.

"Please!" she cried. "Please! I am sorry! I am sorry!"

Her words, of course, fell on the deaf ears of justice. Jennet's mother and brother were quieter, the resignation etched on their weary faces. Like Jennet, they knew that the judge's words were horrid; perhaps the most horrid words they'd ever heard. But they also knew, like Jennet, that they were not unexpected. After all, as Master Nowell had told her, justice had to be done.

Nonetheless, as the reality of the verdicts dawned on her and she watched her family being led out of court for a final time, a dull, empty ache settled into the bottom of Jennet's gut. An ache, she realised, which might never go away.

The court swiftly emptied, the jury retired for a final time and the appetites of the spectators no doubt satiated with the prospect of the public hanging to follow. Jennet remained seated, her gaze cast down, knotting her fingers together as though the repetitive action might ease her dazed agitation. A part of her almost couldn't believe what had just happened, let alone accept her own part in it. Had she really spoken against them; had she really spilled her family's secrets to the court? Had she really just watched them as they were all condemned to die? How could she? How could she have found it in herself to have done these things? As guilty as they were, and as true as every word she had spoken had been, none of it did anything to ease Jennet's conscience.

"Jennet," said a gentle voice, interrupting her whirring, rapid thoughts. "Jennet, it's time to go."

Jennet looked up to see Master Nowell standing over her, his kindly expression once again restored. "You did very well," he said. "It must have been very hard for you."

She nodded, her lip trembling. "I cannot believe that they are all going to die."

"That is justice, I'm afraid," he replied, his expression growing cold. "Justice is not easy, but it is always right. You told the truth and that was the right thing to do. I'm sure that you will come to understand that, one day."

She shook her head, a fog of confusion clouding her thoughts once again. Why was it that Master Nowell's words always seemed to do that to her?

"No matter," he breathed. "What's done is done. It's time to go."

"Go where?" she asked, getting slowly to her feet.

He gave her a small smile. "I promised you that arrangements would be made. I am taking you to your new home."

Jennet's face broke into a grin. She had been so overcome with guilt and grief that she had briefly forgotten about his promise. "Where?" she asked. "Where is my new home?"

"You'll have to wait and see," was all he would tell her.

Jennet followed behind him, a renewed spring finding its way into her step. Giving evidence against her family had been terrible, and watching them be sentenced to their death had been even worse but there was nothing she could do about that now. In time she would heal and in the meantime, she had to remember that she was on her way to her new life, her better life.

"Will I like my new home?" she asked, daring him to tell her more.

"I'm sure you will," he replied. "It is the only place in all the world that you should be."

Yes, she thought, she was certain of it now. He might not want to tell her just yet, but that was only so that he didn't spoil the surprise. She had told the truth, she had helped justice to be done, and now she was to be rewarded. And her reward, she was convinced, was a life at Read Hall with Master Nowell. After all, where else could she go? Read Hall was, as he'd just hinted himself, the only place in the world that she should be.

"Come, child, my horse awaits us. We will need to move quickly if we are to arrive before nightfall," Master Nowell said, taking her by the hand.

As he led her outside and away from Lancaster Castle, Jennet looked over her shoulder, taking in the grim, imposing walls for a final time. She vowed there and then that she would never return to this place. She would leave it in the past, far behind her, along with the spells, the bewitchments, the trials. Along with crumbling stones and days spent by the river. Along with Malkin Tower and her family.

As a guard helped her on to Master Nowell's horse, she allowed herself a small smile. It was time for her future. It was time for comfort, for fine dresses and good food. It was time to be cared for by someone clever, someone who was interested in her. It was time to go to Read Hall, the only place in all the world that she wanted to be.

Epilogue

Summer 1612
'A Father Found'

By the time Master Nowell's horse came to an abrupt halt, it had begun to rain. Jennet watched as the dark grey clouds drew over them, blocking out the evening sunshine and making her shiver. As Master Nowell dismounted she wrapped her arms around herself, his departure leaving her feeling suddenly exposed. Above her the raindrops continued to fall harder and faster, swiftly soaking her skin and her clothes. She let out a heavy sigh and looked around. She felt as though they had been travelling for days, mile upon endless mile spent hunched up on Master Nowell's horse as they rode hard through unfamiliar countryside. Bowland, Master Nowell had called it. The Forest of Bowland. Jennet didn't know where that was, but it sounded a million miles from Pendle.

"Come, Jennet, let's get you down. We walk from here," Master Nowell said.

Jennet clambered down with a heavy groan. "My bones ache," she complained.

Master Nowell let out an amused chuckle. "We have that in common, then," he replied. "But in my case it is because I am no longer a young man, a fact of which I am increasingly aware whenever I must ride. You shall recover quicker than me, I suspect."

Jennet looked around once more. "Where are we? Are we still in Bowland?"

Her questions were met by another cheerful laugh. "No, Jennet. We are almost there. Really, you don't recognise where you are?"

She shook her head. "I've never been here in my life, Master Nowell. Why are we here? I thought..."

He spun around, his gaze growing as dark as the sky above. "You thought what?"

Jennet hesitated before deciding not to share her suspicions just yet. After all, wherever they were right now, it couldn't be far from Pendle. It couldn't be far from Read Hall. Master Nowell clearly wanted to keep her in suspense for as long as possible. "Never mind, Master Nowell. It's nothing," she replied, playing along.

Together they left the lane and walked through the rolling, green fields, Master Nowell's horse trotting obediently at his side. For a man of advancing years Master Nowell walked briskly and although it was a very gentle incline, Jennet quickly found herself completely out of breath. Resolved not to ask any more questions, Jennet occupied herself with her surroundings. Wherever they were, it was very pretty, lush fields full of grazing sheep, interspersed with patches of trees in full bloom. It occurred to her that she had never really studied the countryside around Read Hall; she had spent her time in the library, in her room and in the courtyard, and had been forbidden to wander far. Perhaps this was what the land around Read Hall was like. Perhaps they would reach the top of this incline and it would come into view, sitting there with its grounds, its walls and its finery, waiting for her.

Perhaps this was all just part of the surprise.

"Ah! Here we are," said Master Nowell, interrupting her thoughts. "This place really is quite remote." He pointed ahead of them, towards a small, low cottage nestled into the landscape. Until now, Jennet had barely noticed it, assuming that it was just someone's smallholding, the like of which she had seen many times before. Yet Master Nowell was pointing it out to her. Was this where they were going? And if it was, why?

"What is it?" she asked.

He smiled at her, clearly pleased with himself. "It's your home, Jennet. It's your home - just as I promised."

Jennet felt a flustered heat grow in her cheeks. "But, I don't understand…my home is…it is…"

"It is here," Master Nowell insisted. One sharp look from him was enough to silence her. There were to be no more questions. This was not a matter for discussion. Jennet's stomach gnawed and churned as it sank, along with her heart. The arrangements, she realised, had already been made and, whatever they were, they were not what she had imagined at all.

Master Nowell took her by the hand, pulling her along as they marched the final few paces towards the tiny, grey stone cottage. Without a moment's hesitation he knocked on the wooden door, a regular but insistent tap-tap-tap. No response came from within. Jennet stood and stared ahead of her for what felt like an eternity, studying every crack and flake on the door which, like the rest of this place, was rickety and in dire need of repair. It was nothing like the large, immaculate entrance to Read Hall. But then, she thought with a sad sigh, nowhere in all the world could compare with Master Nowell's grand home.

Jennet flinched as Master Nowell knocked again, abandoning his gentlemanly taps with a loud and urgent banging. "He must be here," he muttered. "I wrote to him and told him I would call today. Ignorant fool probably can't read…"

Jennet's ears pricked up. "Who?" she asked, the question rolling off her tongue before she could stop herself.

"Oh, child! Your father, of course!" Master Nowell snapped, his cheeks reddening.

"My father?" she repeated, her voice little more than a whisper. Master Nowell's harsh tone should have frightened her, but instead all she could think about was what he had said. Her father lived here. Her father; the man she had never known. The part of her life which had never been there.

In that moment, all the world seemed to stop. The wind didn't blow; the clouds didn't roll along in the sky. The rain didn't fall. Time ceased to march on, just for a moment. Just for the briefest moment. Only Jennet's thoughts continued, thoughts of the past and flickers of the future all whirring around her mind. The future she had imagined, and the future she now realised she was actually going to have. A future spent here with a complete stranger - that was what Master Nowell had meant by arrangements. She felt the heat of tears pricking behind her eyes. Master Nowell had never planned to take her home with him. What a fool she had been.

Master Nowell banged hard on the door once more, and this time his call was answered. As the door creaked open, Jennet caught a first glimpse of the man who was her father. She had to crane her neck to look up at him as he was very tall, his posture slightly awkward as he held himself under the low roof of his cottage. For a moment Jennet studied him intently, taking in his features which were striking and dark. It occurred to her that he was exactly how her sister had once described him, when she had asked.

"He's very tall with brown hair and brown eyes," she'd said. "Far too tall for Mother! Goodness knows what she saw in him."

The memory made Jennet shudder and she pushed it from her mind. Her sister was dead; those were the words of a ghost now. Little wonder they made her blood run cold.

The man caught her eye and gave her a smile. "Hello, Jennet," he said with a brief nod. Jennet looked away. She couldn't bring herself to speak to him, not yet.

"Richard Sellers," Master Nowell began, his voice loud and filled once again with authority. "I presume you received my letter?"

Richard nodded. "Aye," he said quietly. "I have heard what happened at the assizes. Folk can talk of nothing else around these parts. A terrible business, terrible business indeed."

Master Nowell gave Richard Sellers a keen, disapproving stare.

"What happened was justice, Goodman Sellers. But justice does have consequences, as I stated in my letter…" he allowed his voice to trail off, but his gesture towards Jennet made his point clear enough.

Richard sighed, his gaze returning to the girl standing before him. "Aye of course, the child is without a mother now."

"But not a father," Master Nowell was quick to add. "The time has come to assume some responsibility Goodman Sellers, in repentance for your sins, if nothing else."

Richard gave Master Nowell a hard stare. "The girl is not a sin. I'd have wed her mother, if she'd have had me. It was her choice to raise the child alone."

Master Nowell greeted his explanation with a dismissive flick of his hand. "None of this concerns me. I am simply here to bring you what is yours."

His cold tone made the tears well up in Jennet's eyes all over again. Her heart broke at the way he spoke of her, as though she was an object, something to be traded. As though she was nothing at all. "Master Nowell," she began. "Master Nowell, please…I…please…" She moved towards him, clasping her hands together as her mind reeled, trying to put what she wanted to say to him into words, to tell him how much she wanted to live with him, how happy it would make her. But the words wouldn't come. "Please don't leave me here." That was all she could manage: a feeble, final, desperate plea.

Before Master Nowell could answer her, Richard Sellers intervened. "Come on, child," he said gently, bending down so that his face was level with hers. "No point in begging a gentleman - no good ever comes of that. I'll see that you're well taken care of. You'll have a good life here; I promise you that." He stretched out his long arms, gathering her in towards him. "It's good to finally meet you, Jennet, despite the circumstances."

"You see," said Master Nowell, his tone triumphant. "Just as I promised you, Jennet. A better life, spent exactly where you should be."

Still caught up in those huge arms, Jennet could do little more than nod. Something about Richard's warm, fatherly embrace softened Jennet's resolve. Her head still wanted her to scream and shout, to tell Master Nowell that this was all wrong, that he must take her with him. Her heart, however, responded to the affection this man had shown towards her, to the tenderness and care promised by his words. He was her father, after all. He might not be the father she wanted, but he was the one she had. After everything that had happened, after everyone that she had lost and the part she had played in losing them, it occurred to Jennet that she was fortunate to have anyone at all.

"I'll be on my way, then," Master Nowell said, giving them both a final brusque glance before taking hold of his horse once more.

Richard Sellers stood up, giving Master Nowell a deferential nod. "Thank you, Sir," he said. "Thank you for bringing her to me."

Master Nowell simply smiled. "Well, where else would I have taken her?" he scoffed. "I could hardly have taken her home with me! That would have been most…unseemly."

Jennet's heart lurched into her mouth at Master Nowell's careless mockery. If only he knew how her hopes and dreams had kept her going all these months, how they had given her the strength to do what he had asked of her. If only he knew the pain which his disregard caused her now.

"Goodbye, Jennet," Master Nowell said, before turning away for a final time.

"Goodbye, Master Nowell," she muttered, her voice hoarse and strained from the effort of suppressed tears. She watched as he simply walked away. He had no smile for her, no parting embrace or gesture, or even a glance. He had nothing for her now. She had done his bidding. She had outlived her usefulness. And now he had discarded her without a second thought.

"I am unseemly," she whispered as Master Nowell disappeared into the distance. The unfamiliar syllables felt strange on her tongue. She would commit the word to memory, placing it alongside all those other words she had heard about herself over the years: a bastard, a little wench, a poor wretch. It was just a word, just another word capable of shattering her spirit.

"No, you aren't," Richard Sellers said from behind her. For a moment she had almost forgotten he was there. "But he is a gentleman – he's no good for the likes of us. That's something you'll have to learn, Jennet." He placed a protective hand upon her shoulder and to her surprise, Jennet found that she appreciated the gesture.

"He never even left the bodice and petticoat he gave me. He promised I could keep them. I loved that petticoat," Jennet lamented, the tears streaming down her cheeks. Before she could stop herself she turned and hugged her father, holding on tight to this stranger, this man she barely knew. At any other time, the absurdity of it would have made her cheeks flush with embarrassment, but she was so overcome with grief, so possessed by the need for comfort that at that moment, she didn't care.

"Oh, lass," Richard said, patting her gently on the back. "I can't promise you fine clothes like that, but I will care for you. Truth be told, I don't really know how to be a father, but I promise you that I will do my very best."

Jennet gave a meek nod. "It's not just the petticoat," she sniffed. "I've lost everything. Everything I had and everything I wanted – it's all gone. You know what I did, don't you? You know what Master Nowell asked me to do, you know what I said…?'"

"Aye, I know," he replied. "I know what the likes of Nowell and the other sheriffs have been up to as well. Witch trials in Lancaster, witch trials in York, both assizes full to bursting with poor, unfortunate folk, almost all of whom were sent to the gallows. For Christian men it seems to me they've a lot of blood on their hands."

Jennet frowned, the flicker of a memory of something Master Nowell had said at the assizes returning to her. "I heard about the York assizes but I don't know what happened there. I wondered if it had anything to do with my mother's friend, Jennet Preston."

"Aye, that's right," her father replied with a nod. "Tried and acquitted at the Lent assizes for witchcraft, but I hear she wasn't so lucky the second time around."

"Jennet's eyes widened. "You mean she's…?"

Her father nodded slowly. "That's right. Sent to the gallows for bewitching to death Master Lister of Westby Hall."

"But Jennet loved Master Lister. She wouldn't have killed him. I remember Mama was so cross with his son for wanting to see Jennet hang just because she loved his father…" Jennet bit her lip, stemming the flow of her words as she remembered what she had testified to in court. She had told Master Nowell all of this, of course, and all of her words had been used as evidence. Including, no doubt, against Jennet Preston. Poor kind, gentle Jennet Preston. She hadn't deserved to die.

"Aye well, as I said to you, no good comes of associating with gentlemen. Listers, Nowells, they're all the same."

A pang of guilt reverberated through Jennet's chest. It was starting to dawn on her just how true that was.

"Things will be different now, Jennet, not like they were before. But time will help, you'll see. It will get easier."

"Will it?" she asked, feeling unsure. She was suddenly so tired, so confused. So overwhelmed.

Her father gave her a measured look. "You've a lot to come to terms with, lass. You might not understand that now, but you will. Try to think of today as a new beginning, the start of a new life. Try to put everything that happened before today in the past, where it belongs."

Several large spots of rain landed on Jennet's skin, warning of more heavy rainfall to come. Richard invited her to come inside, giving her a first glimpse of the humble cottage which was to be her home. For a moment she hovered in the doorway, feeling uneasy in these unfamiliar surroundings, unsure how to be or where to put herself.

"You'll get used to it," her father said, taking her gently by the hand. "It's your home now. You're safe here, Jennet."

Jennet nodded. It was true; no matter how she felt now, it was indeed her home, and the start of her new life. It wasn't what she had imagined for herself, or what had filled her dreams for months on end but given everything that had happened, and everything that she had done, it was perhaps far more than she deserved. She studied the cottage, absorbing its every detail; its tired stone walls, its sparse furnishings, its rickety chairs draped with worn blankets. Although it was much smaller, it reminded her of somewhere else, somewhere she used to live in a previous life. Somewhere she should now consign to the past. Somewhere it would be better to forget.

She knew, of course, that forgetting would be easier said than done. As young as she was, she realised it would take all the strength she could muster not to succumb to the guilt which already gnawed at her, not to be haunted by the ghosts of the past. But she had to try. Her family had perished, but she had survived. In a strange sort of way, she felt she owed it to them to go on, to try to make something of her life, to try not to be consumed by the same fate which found them. If she could manage that, then perhaps in time her guilt might ease. Perhaps.

Jennet looked up at her father, a small smile breaking on her face. "Thank you," she said.

Richard Sellers furrowed his brow. "For what?"

Jennet shrugged, trying to formulate her gratitude into some sensible words. "For taking me in, I suppose. For not leaving me alone. I hate being alone more than anything."

Richard gave her a sad smile. "Aye, me too," he replied. "But if there is any good to come from all of this, it is that neither of us shall ever be alone again."

He drew her close, holding on to her as though his strong embrace might be able to make up for a lifetime spent apart. Jennet clung to him, indulging herself in the feeling of being safe, of being protected, of being loved. Of having a father. Feelings which she had wanted to enjoy for as long as she could remember. She knew deep down that it was more than she deserved, yet fate had thrown them together anyway. In that brief moment everything that had happened - the deaths of her grandmother, her mother, her brother and her sister, the dreadful role she'd played in it all – faded into insignificance, leaving her with a strange serenity, a sense that she was the luckiest girl in the world.

Of course, as quickly as it had arrived the feeling passed, leaving in its place that familiar ache of guilt and loss. Her father was right; she had a lot to come to terms with, a lot to accept and even more to punish herself for. She knew already that her future was not going to be easy, but at least she wouldn't have to face it alone.

For all the trouble he had brought to her, for all the things he had taken away, Master Nowell had at least given her one parting gift. Whether he had meant to or not, he had given her someone who cared for her, someone who wanted her. He had given her a father. Above all, she thought, he had given her someone who, probably for the first time in her life, would make sure that she never felt alone again.

Richard released her from his firm embrace, studying her expression with big, concerned eyes. "Are you going to be alright?" he asked.

Jennet nodded. "I hope so," she replied, and she meant it. She wanted to be alright; maybe not today or tomorrow but one day, when she'd laid enough ghosts to rest, suffered enough sleepless nights, felt enough grief and self-loathing. She just needed to give it time. After all, her father had said that time would help her. At that moment, she hoped more than anything that he was right.

The End

AUTHOR'S NOTES

This novella is a story about Jennet Device, the youngest daughter of Elizabeth Device and granddaughter of Elizabeth Southerns, alias Old Demdike, who were both accused of witchcraft in the Pendle witch hunt of 1612. Born in 1600 and therefore aged almost twelve when the trials took place, Jennet is remembered by history as the child witness, the small girl who stood on a bench and delivered the damning testimony which sent her mother, brother, sister and countless others to the gallows.

This story began its life as part of my second Witches of Pendle novel, *A Woman Named Sellers*, which focusses on the adult life of Jennet Device, a woman haunted by her past who finds herself caught up in Pendle's second wave of witch trials in the 1630s. It quickly became apparent to me, however, that her childhood story deserved a separate space in which to be told. It is a story which is filled with complexity, with trauma, and with tragedy, and one which ultimately hinges on one question: why would a little girl turn against her own family and give evidence which condemned them all to hang? It is this question which this novella tries to answer, reading between the lines of the historical facts to analyse the psychology of a young girl living over four hundred years ago, reared in rural isolation, superstition and dire poverty. I must say that as a writer, it was one of the most challenging I have ever tried to do.

The court records of the time, though laden with propaganda and bias, were also meticulous. They provide a wealth of information about the events which reportedly took place in the years leading up to the witch trials, the crimes the Devices were accused of, and the evidence Jennet ultimately gave, and I used these details faithfully when crafting this story. At times I have conflated some events or amended the timeline slightly to suit the narrative, and to ensure consistency with the first two novels which cover some of the same subject matter. For example, the records suggest that the altercation with the miller Baldwin took place in

1610, with his daughter dying a year later. In *The Gisburn Witch* I brought these two events closer together for impact and immediacy; therefore, they are similarly presented in this novella.

The court records also hint at some of the familial conflicts in the Device household, which were useful in developing this story. For example, we know from evidence given at the 1612 trials that there was some question over Jennet's legitimacy, and that it was widely believed that she was the daughter of a man named Sellers. I pursued this theory concerning Jennet's parentage in my first two Witches of Pendle novels, *The Gisburn Witch* and *A Woman Named Sellers*. In this novella I have explored it further, framing it as a key source of tension within the Device household and a damaging blow to Jennet's sense of self, fuelling feelings of being lonely and unloved. This is, of course, entirely fictional but given the sensational stand she made against her family during the trials it seems plausible that she felt set apart from the rest of them, as well as understandably horrified at their perceived witchcraft. We also cannot know for certain that following the trials Jennet went to live with her father. However, this assertion is supported by some historical evidence: in 1635, a Jennet Sellers alias Device was buried in Newchurch-in-Pendle. If this was the same Jennet, then at the very least the evidence suggests that after 1612 father and daughter grew close enough that she felt able to adopt his surname.

In order to create the story, I wove a number of other fictional elements in amongst the factual background to the 1612 trials. Between her family's arrest in the spring and the trials in the summer, we don't know exactly where Jennet resided, and we cannot be certain about the interactions which took place between herself and Roger Nowell, although as the local magistrate he undoubtedly interviewed her. Given her position as star witness for the prosecution, however, it is hard not to think that she spent those months living at Read Hall in the company of Master Nowell. Given also the impressive nature of her testimony, it is easy to imagine his influence over her, first in persuading her of the importance of giving evidence, and then in coaching her on how to frame her answers for the jury. Jennet was, after all, only a young girl; poor, uneducated and impressionable. How awe-inspiring that gentleman, his fine home and his clever ideas must have seemed to her.

If this novella has inspired an interest in the Pendle Witch Trials, I can recommend two good books on the subject. These are *The Lancashire Witch Craze: Jennet Preston and the Lancashire Witches, 1612* by Jonathan Lumby and *The Lancashire Witch Conspiracy: A History of Pendle Forest and the Pendle Witch Trials* by John A Clayton. It is also worth reading the only primary source which exists concerning the 1612 trials in Lancaster: *The Wonderfull Discoverie of Witches in the Countie of Lancaster* written by the court clerk, Thomas Potts.

ABOUT THE AUTHOR

Sarah L King lives in West Lothian, Scotland, with her husband and young children. Born in Nottingham and raised in Lancashire, Sarah spent much of her childhood captivated by Pendle witch folklore. The Pendle Witch Girl is the third book in her Witches of Pendle series, accompanying The Gisburn Witch (2015) and A Woman Named Sellers (2016).

In addition to her historical fiction novels, in 2017 Sarah published a contemporary novel, Ethersay, a mystery/women's fiction/political fiction hybrid set during the Scottish independence referendum in 2014.

When she's not writing Sarah loves long country walks, romantic ruins, Thai food and spending time with her family.

For further information please visit her website & blog at http://www.sarahlking.com/

Printed in Great Britain
by Amazon